MW01632266

Front cover art: Online Pictures
Chapter insets: Talmadge Moose
Design and typesetting: Ted Wojtasik

Acknowledgements
"St. Elvis of Tupelo, Pray for Us," by Susie Paul was first published in The Village Rambler, *Pittsboro, NC.*

ISBN-13: 978-0999787366
ISBN-10: 0999787365

St. Andrews Press

St. Andrews University
(A Branch of Webber International University)
1700 Dogwood Mile
Laurinburg, NC 28352
press@sa.edu
(910) 277-5310

Also by Ruth Moose

Poetry

To Survive

Finding Things in the Dark

Making the Bed

Smith Grove

Tea and Other Poems

The Librarian

Fiction

The Wreath Ribbon Quilt and Other Stories

Dreaming in Color

Neighbors and Other Strangers

Doing it at the Dixie Dew

Wedding Bell Blues

Editor

I Have Walked: an Anthology on Poverty

Twelve Christmas Stories by North Carolina Writers

Women's Fiction from Potato Eyes

Dedicated to

Talmadge Moose
wherever he is

St. Elvis of Tupelo, Pray for Us

Susie Paul

Pray for us, St. Elvis of
sky-suede shoes, of
spangled suits, of
moon-blank Lycra, the stretched
expanse clean
as pearly new paper.

Bless us, Elvis of pelvis
swiveling,so like
our gyrating earth, plump planet,
tipped upon its axis
spine, veering and unveering
as it loves the sun.

Intercede for us, Elvis of
Tupelo, we mothers of
anarchic sons, we who persevere
when fathers fear and flee, or fade, or
cannot
face themselves remade
in a world they could not
fix.

Intercede for us, Elvis, through
whom God cherishes
the will-not-be-controlled,
recalcitrant and mutineers.
Intercede for us with
Jesus of the rock-
and-roll heart, who disrespected
elders, hit the road, howled
half-naked in the desert, hallucinating
devils, feared His own grown-
up destiny. Who hung with ne'er-do-wells

and malcontents, fishermen in
sandals, lepers, cheats, and
Pharisees, kids clamoring, the un-
dead, and attentive, easy women, calling—
Leave it all behind, mother, father, sister,
brother, their ancient expectations. Leave,
and follow me away
from following.

Pray for us, St. Elvis of Tupelo,
born of Gladys in a crazy-legged house,
reared in Memphis, wrapped
around your twin expiring, you twisted out
on stillborn heels, Elvis Aron, high
priest earth angel god of gaudy
Bibled bandit potentate
of plush. Pray
for us, deliverer
of trashy persons everywhere.
Teach us to give
our own kewpies Cadillacs,
to face them,
the fan and the offended
with arch eyebrow,
furled lip.
Teach us
to face it with
hip.

Table of Contents

Prologue

Pilgrims All

In August, in the South, when day here boils over into the night and there's a hard ring around the moon, those who believe go seeking Salvation. They are tired of waiting for The Rapture. If The Rapture is not going to come to them, they will pick up their lives where they are, pack a lunch and go to it. They pack brown grocery bags full of Nabs, cans of Spam and Vienna Sausages, pork and beans. They take along very carefully, packed in its own Tupperware keeper, Aunt Ophelia's Caramel Pound Cake with inches thick Burnt Sugar Icing. They pack ham biscuits, fried chicken and deviled eggs that smell to high heaven. Last, they put in a watermelon big as a half-bushel bucket. They throw in a change of underwear and head toward where The Rapture is. They go to Graceland. They go to ask the blessings of their lord and savior, Elvis the King.

At the gates of Graceland, they stand, The Secretary in her green suit with her driver and angels-on-the-hood car. The Bookstore Clerk with his mother-in-law and child calling "Cedora, Cedora, are you in there? Won't you come home?" They have prayed this prayer each night for three years. They know Cedora will come back to them if Elvis says the word.

The Dutiful Daughter, Clemmie Rink, with her old cat in her arms, waits there telling her mama to hold her horses. It's almost opening time. She can't wait to get into Graceland and eat some of those fried peanut butter and banana sandwiches with Elvis. Yum, yum.

There's Treena with another quilt bundled in her arms like a child. She wants Elvis to heal the hole in her son's heart. She knows Him, and He alone can come up with this miracle.

Motoring Mable, The Hairdresser, stands there with her blowers and combs, scissors, curlers, and sprays. She just wants to get her hands on Elvis' magic locks. She wants to feel that wonderful hair on her fingers. She is sure He will recognize her talent and let her travel with Him wherever He goes. She does not ever want to go back where she was.

There stands Dixie Vanilla, who wrestled her way to the top, stopped by a car wash on her way to Graceland. She knows Elvis appreciates a Cadillac, and all the work she had done on her baby didn't come cheap. Elvis will admire her car. And she can't wait to tell Him how her Cadillac performed when she used it like a tank. Why, honey, nothing could touch that thing until a cop stopped her. She wants Elvis to hang her manager, that cheating Clifford T., on a cross and let crows pluck every hair from his head, every whisker from his chin, every last lash from his eyes, every sprig of tuft from his armpits to his legs. She wants him bald and clean and full of remorse.

Revis Ames, The Retired Shoe Salesman, is there with his car full of empty jars of homemade scuppernong wine. His trip has been one long drinking and singing party, but he saved one quart for Elvis to bless.

Drayton Brewster stands with Helen on his arm, all smiles. He wears new white suede shoes and is ready to dance. Helen calls him her Teddy Bear. He's been putting his weight back on from all Helen's good chocolate cakes and he wants to thank Elvis for helping him pull up his pants and put back on his life.

Preacher Tovin Ellis is there on his motorcycle. He wears black and his heart is heavy for his sweet little wife who left him for someone else. Someone who does not believe. The preacher will ask Elvis to heal his heart. To restore his faith so he may minister to others. He will ask Elvis to help him be faithful to his calling all his life and to love his congregation even when they try his patience and rub him wrong. But most of all he wants his wife back. He is willing to do anything Elvis says, go anywhere Elvis says to go. All he wants is Joyce, Joyce, Joyce.

Aunt Lottie, The Sister, is there to pray for Uncle Drum to get some sense in his gray head. She knows this Dove woman is looking for gold. The woman even painted her nails with it. Lottie knows a woman with ten-inch claws when she sees her.

Chalmers Dewitt, The Widower, is in line and already has his ticket. It's his Free Pass. The guard at the gate says he has never seen such as this. Is it legal? Legal as your left arm, Dewitt says and pokes The Preacher in the side. The pass is edged in gold with a seal as big as an orange. It looks official. The guard calls another and they look at the signature. The other guard says that's E's signature, I'd know it across the room. He wets his finger and the ink doesn't run. Go on in, he says, Elvis is in here.

There's a redheaded woman with Him and she told us you'd come looking. The Banker's Wife comes to find her soul. She sold it too low and will pay anything now to get it back. She couldn't find joy if it grew on a stalk in front of her nose. She cannot sleep until she gets her soul back to put at the foot of her bed.

The Professor brings the skin of a red fox to give Elvis. She knows He loves animals. She also brings a box of the bones of her marriage. She wants Elvis to raise it from the dead. She knows He can do it.

The Artist wants his reputation restored and his neighbor destroyed. He is not sorry for what he did and still wants her to pay. He promises to paint all of the flowers that grow in Graceland's gardens before he is done.

Three Women from the garden club come as a group to ask Elvis to find their friend's diamond ring so they can have peace in the place they live.

Then there is The New Woman who left her husband at the beach hotel. She left him with his TV clicker and not much else. She wants to be missed a lot. She wants to be assured everything will be different if she ever darkens the door of her marriage again.

The Family wants Elvis to tell them his favorite joke and they will tell him what it means. They collect jokes like some people collect coins. Except theirs are free.

Miss Lettie Broom, The Single Woman, is there. She almost took up with an insurance man who is married. She wants Elvis to tell him to leave his wife and run back to her. She promises never to burn biscuits again.

The Country Girl is there with her fiancée. She wants to thank Elvis for helping her find love in the city. She has a smile as big as the moon. She wants Elvis to bless them and marry them. That way they will be happy forever.

The pilgrims at Graceland's Gates wait for an audience with Elvis. Is he in there? Surely Elvis hasn't left this building. Surely, he will always be here. Always.

The Mother's Story

Waiting for Elvis

Before Blaine Boyd was born, I started my first quilt, not knowing what I was doing any more than a cat trying to crochet. I knew I had to be off my feet, and if I didn't do something to keep my hands busy and my mind off things, I'd lose it. My mind and the baby.

Avalona, my mother-in-law, claims that's when it started. She'd put guilt on me as heavy as a lead jacket if I let her. But I don't, and I won't. I did everything I could and nothing she has ever said is going to make me believe it's my fault, something in my doing or not doing that made Blaine Boyd the way he is. God made him and Elvis. Elvis, who has been there and back and walks this earth every day, is going to unmake him and make him right.

I believe that. No matter what Elvis sang, it was like he knew I was listening. He sang straight to me. He could be in Las Vegas or overseas or the Grand Old Opry or anywhere at all and he sang to me. I felt it. I still feel it. Sometimes I listen and listen to all his songs for some message. Some word that will tell me where he is. Blaine Boyd listens too.

If it was up to me and Blaine Boyd, we would have taken out on the road long ago. I keep telling him we will know when. There will be a sign. I don't know what the sign will be, but I'm sure I will when I see it. In the meantime, we wait. Blaine's waited so long, he's almost forgotten how to do anything else. Not that he was ever able to do much. From the minute he was born, he was always the quietest child.

"Such a good baby," everybody said.

"Too good," Franklin's mother, Avalona Boyd, said. "It's not natural." We didn't tell her for the longest time, but she knew. She always said there hadn't been anybody born who could put much past her for long. Blaine was born with a hole in his heart big as a fist and all the sewing and patching he's had isn't going to last forever.

Avalona said, "That baby's color is as blue as skim milk." She said that standing like a wicked witch right over his crib. That's one time I grabbed her by the elbow and hustled her out as fast as I could. She spluttered and spit like a wet setting hen, "Well, I never. Thrown out of my own son's house like a hussy." She hissed the last word and it slid around the door and forked into my face. But I'd do it again. A baby like Blaine Boyd didn't need that kind of talk around him, and I wasn't going to put up with it from Franklin's mama or anybody else. She should have had more sense, but then she's always been Avalona.

Way before I married Franklin, back when I worked at the Cinderella Knitting Mills, people told me, "Honey, Franklin may be an all right fellow, but I wouldn't wish Avalona Boyd for a mother-in-law on my worst enemy."

Avalona cried when we told her we were engaged. "You're taking my baby," she said, "I got nothing left."

I just stood there not knowing what to say, feeling like I'd done something I shouldn't have but didn't know what.

Then Franklin's daddy, Joe Dean, said in his shy little way, "You still got me, 'Lona.'" She turned and looked at him like she saw him for the first time and she didn't know who he was nor where he'd come from. But she didn't stop crying until Franklin himself hugged and kissed her.

Now Franklin's moved back in with her and I should have seen it coming. From the first, I should have seen the whole picture spread out in front of me like a billboard spelling out: "Every Day is Mother's Day."

I see Franklin's truck when he comes home from work every day and when it leaves every morning. I see him come out the back door with his little rolled-up lunch bag and thermos of milk. She must still think he's in kindergarten. She never did think I pampered his ulcer enough. I think if a man's got an ulcer, you don't make it better nagging and reminding him. Not a grown man, at least. If Franklin ever reaches the place where he is such a thing, I hope I'm around to see it. Not that I begrudge his love for his mother. That's something I admire and respect. It's hard to see that and not say something. Sometimes I think I've said too much and they're up at their house next door watching me like I'm watching them.

Every day is Mother's Day with me and Blaine, who is as sweet as he is good. It's been that way for nine years now.

Sometimes I can't believe it, but then I look at all the quilts, though he claims his kitty cat one is the best I ever made. I put red-plaid cats on it, orange polka dot cats, green striped cats ... you name it. But I wouldn't put a black cat on it. Not that I'm superstitious; I just didn't want to change a thing. Not when I've got so much going on right now. I think if I put all the quilts I've made end to end, side by side, I could walk them and be halfway to Graceland and back. Add to that the ones I've helped cut out and pieced a block to show how or quilted a row to show you can get ten stitches to an inch ifyou know what you're doing.

And I do. I ought to, as much time and thought and doing as I've done on quilts the last ten years. They've saved my life, I can tell you.

"Honey boy," I told Blaine, sitting there with his kitty-cat quilt and big eyes, "we got two good minds going for us here and—"

"Mawmaw's only got one," he said and giggled, covering his mouth with both hands like he was catching them as they spilled out.

"I didn't say that." I wet the tip of my finger and tested the steam iron. The only way to check is the old-fashioned way mama taught me. That's what I've taught everybody in my quilting classes. You press as much as you stitch if you want to turn out something you're proud of. From the tip of your finger to the last seam, you check your work. The iron was hot but not too hot. It was okay for cotton, but not satin. When I get my hands on that white satin, it will be a different story. I imagine how it will feel, cool as water, smooth and falling like a bank of snow behind my iron.

The first thing I'll do when I get my wedding dress back is to take it apart piece by piece, then pick out every stitch. And I'll think while I'm doing it how I'm picking out of my life every ugly word Avalona Boyd or her son ever thought or said in my direction. But first I have to get my wedding dress back. It's not like I'm stealing it. If anything, it belongs to me, that dress does. Trouble is, that dress lies high and hard to get in a big Belk's box way up in Avalona Boyd's attic. And she's got the key. And my husband. Of the two right now, I'd rather have the dress, but if I can get one, I'll be on my way to getting the other.

Blaine folded up his blanket and turned off the TV. Sometimes he leaned over the back of the couch and just looked out the window for the longest kind of time. He knew the rest of the kids were in school, his daddy was at work and lord only knows what his grandmother was up to. I would leave my sewing or the ironing board and look over his shoulder trying to see what he saw, but it was just woods and the road, maybe birds or squirrels or wind-blowing leaves. Blaine watched the road like he looked for somebody to come down it. Somebody or something that would save him and change our lives. I got my own ideas.

Even if I never had an art lesson in my life, I can draw what I like. Of course, I have to look at something to get my ideas, then go from there but people can tell what it is.

"Lord, Treena," they always say, "you got talent."

I used to say, why anybody could do it if they wanted. Then I saw just anybody couldn't. I saw what some people drew and cut out and called flowers but it didn't look any more like flowers than a sack of cloth. So I quit saying that and kept on drawing my patterns and making my one-of-a-kind quilts, which they are anyway, if you think about it. I always have to add things, "touches" to patterns I get from books. My Sunbonnet Sue quilt has lace on her step-ins and bows on her dress, wee tiny doll buttons on her high-top shoes. I worked it out sitting in the hospital by Blaine's bed. Saw the pictures in my mind and drew it on paper, then pieced most of it before he came home. He liked to look over and see what I was working on.

Now we're working on the Elvis quilt, and he says that's going to be the best of all. That we will go on Oprah and show the quilt and Elvis will see it wherever he is and come and give him a new heart.

Why not? Elvis gave people things like brand new Cadillac cars and stuff. A brand-new heart is way above that. Why, Elvis can just write a check or say a word to the right doctor and Blaine Boyd will have his new heart and the rest of our lives will be like this never happened.

So, I'm trying to be ready. To get the Elvis quilt pieced and quilted, and when the time comes the miracle will be there waiting with our names on it.

The same as my wedding dress in Avalona Boyd's attic. It has my name on it and every stitch in it is mine. I could go buy white satin, but Franklin puts money under the big rock by the driveway every Saturday morning—it wouldn't work. The white satin suit for Elvis on the quilt has to be made of something that belonged to me and I am giving up. It has to have my memories, my tears, my hopes and dreams, the feel of me made to fit him. That's what will make it work.

So early in the morning and late at night, I thought of ways to break into my mother-in-law's house and pull down those creaky disappearing stairs, grab that box and fly out the door like a thief, which I am not.

When I saw in the paper that an Elvis Impersonator was to be at the mall, I knew I could not wait any longer. I had to get my dress, finish the quilt in time to give it to Elvis at the mall. The ad might say impersonator, but I would know. I would know if this was really Elvis or an Elvis wannabe, or a dressed-up trying to be Elvis.

So I hatched up a plan with Blaine Boyd and we played like I was his MawMaw and what he'd say and do, and he knew what I was saying and doing the whole time.

Blaine Boyd was to sit on the front steps of his grandmother's house and cry. Cry like he had never cried before. He was to tell her he didn't know where his mother was. That I had been gone when he got up that morning. And if she insisted, and I knew she would, on going down to the trailer to look for me, he was to show her my good made up bed and my note that said I loved him. And while he was with her, I was digging up the extra backdoor key she had wrapped in aluminum foil and buried under a rock, letting myself into the house and up the attic stair. Which all went as planned except for the coffee pot. Blaine Boyd said she got suspicious when she saw a full pot of fresh coffee on the stove. Avalona knew that I knew there wasn't a coffee pot in the world she could pass without sitting down to have at least one cup. It was a trap I'd laid to delay her right then and there. Which she knew. Not that it did her any good. Blaine Boyd said she poured herself a cup and inspected my kitchen while she drank it. He said she looked in every cabinet, my refrigerator, the oven and even poked around under my sink, which I will have you know is clean as my counter on top. By that time Avalona had finished the whole pot. Then she left a note for me, "Good to the last drop. A." Which I didn't know if she meant the coffee or herself. Anyway, I barely got the box, let the attic stairs lifted back into place good and made it out the back door. I got the key buried again when I heard her come in the front. I took off like the scared cat I really am.

I had to cut and sew all night making my life-size Elvis in his white satin suit. That left me four days and nights to quilt the borders in a diamond pattern. I'd used pale blue and silver for the background. I had to embroider his face, cut a microphone out of black cloth. I even left the cord loose, so it would look real and made Elvis' long eyelashes from black thread. When I finished, he was so handsome he almost took my breath away.

It was four in the morning when I tied the last knot behind the last rhinestone. I spread the quilt out on my bed and woke Blaine Boyd to come and see. He just rubbed his eyes, then grinned and reached me the biggest hug. "It's him, Mama," he said. "It's him all right."

We stood there hugging, half-laughing, half-crying. Blaine Boyd all warm and sleepy against me and me so tired I was crazy.

I knew Blaine Boyd could never stand the excitement of the crowd and the noise, so we took one last look at that quilt before I rolled it up like a big fat, puffy, shiny log that lay light on my back seat as I drove to the mall.

There were posters of Elvis everywhere I looked, and since the show didn't start until eight and I got there at six, I got a front row seat. Right next to two women so fat their bodies billowed out over both sides of the little folding chairs in front of that stage. A little girl, about six or seven, sat first on one's lap, then the other's. Fonda Kay, the woman called her. I never did find out which one was her mama. Fonda Kay, they said, had been to ten of these Elvis impersonator concerts and always gave him a rose. She held, in my face, a long-stemmed red silk twisted little flower on a green wire with a couple of leaves. It smelled like the inside of one of these cheap stores where they sell candy and mothballs and cleaning products, and everything gets to smell a little bit of the same.

Before long every chair was filled, and the whole mall started to hum like a hive of busy bees. Someone would say, "Here he comes," and the talk rose to a fever pitch. Nothing happened and there would be some quietness for a little bit. Then the hum picked up again. I sat there with my quilt on my lap and thought maybe the whole thing was a hoax, a come-on to get people out to the mall, and all my work and hurry and staying up late at night had been for nothing.

Next thing I knew, there he was: Elvis. Only this time he had on a red satin jumpsuit and two twitty blonde girls with him, all carrying guitars. They were pale as clouds and had broomstick figures, but big hair and caked-on makeup. He swung around the cord to his mike and started in, but before the first note came out of his mouth, I knew this was no Elvis impersonator. This was Elvis. Capital E Elvis. The real McCoy. I almost giggled. The whole disguise was just perfect. What better way to hide from the public and still keep doing the thing you do best but impersonate yourself. I knew because the first thing Elvis did when the heel of his boot came down on that stage was wink at me. Quick and sly, and if I hadn't been all stretched up and ready for it, I would have missed that eye blink, it was so quick.

I didn't hear, nor see anything after that. Just hugged my quilt roll and waited for him to wind down. Which he did, after "Hound Dog" and throwing scarves out to the crowd and leaning down to kiss the little girl, Fonda Kay, when her mother held her up. She kept the rose. Probably the same old rose she'd taken to see him ten times. What would he want with a tacky old flower when he was going to get the most beautiful quilt in the world? And pinned to that quilt was my letter with my name, address, and phone number, asking for Blaine Boyd's new heart.

When Elvis left the stage, I was ready. As he brushed by, I laid that quilt in his arms like a baby. He didn't even slow his stride, but took it and went on, the crowd swirling after him.

It wasn't long before I lost sight of the back of his head and the turned-up collar of that red jumpsuit. I didn't need anything else. I knew he knew that I knew. He was the real Elvis and he'd call before I got home.

I hurried to my car and didn't even stay for the fireworks which were going off right and left as I pulled out of the parking lot.

A tall white flame shot all silver and gold into the sky and rained down stars. I said to myself, "That's you and me and Elvis, Blaine Boyd. We'll hit the charts with our new heart." I laughed. The slogan was so catchy I said it over and over as I gave the car more gas and roared toward home.

The Retired Salesman's Story

Mercury Vapors

Revis Ames woke to the sound of someone crying.

"Mama," the voices said, but they didn't sound like his children. Moonlight softened the shapes of his bedposts, bulky bear of a cedar wardrobe and dresser with a triangle smudge of gray lamp in the mirror. He didn't have his glasses on, but he knew this room. Knew it top to bottom, mattress to door. Knew the summer dust smell of it, the winter cold sharp cut of it and the green growing spring nights like now. Knew the emptiness of half his bed and how he still couldn't sleep on her side of it, fit into the hollow she left.

"Mama," the voices sang again.

"Oh JesusgodOmama." They tuned up like a chorus.

He felt under his mattress for the pistol and couldn't find it. He swore and reached so deep he stretched a muscle in his arm until it twinged. Still no pistol. Whoever they were in his front yard carrying on like crazy. And with all that racket, they probably wouldn't be sneaking and quiet. Not hollering for all the world to hear. The worst thief had made no sound at all. He knew that thief. Knew him well.

With his feet he felt for his shoes and found one of hers, flat and soft as a cat. He pushed it away, then felt the solid block of his own, slipped into them and even tied the laces in the dark. Funny, the things you could do by feel even if your hands are a little shaky.

"OhhhhhhLord," the voices cried.

Revis reached his shirt off the bedpost and slipped into it, then his pants, which he zipped and belted. Then he felt one more time for the gun before he opened the bedroom door and stepped into the hall. For all he knew, that crying could be the wind, a storm coming up and his imagination working hard to keep him company. But he knew it wasn't. No wind ever said, "Mama." Not like that. And besides, he thought, as he stood in the hall, there wasn't any wind. He didn't even hear the little bud leaves on the trees moving.

Outside, and through the living room windows, the moon rode low and flat like a home-weary horse.

The crying stopped and he heard a car door slam. Then a groan and someone talking.

He didn't know what time it was, but it felt like some little hour in the morning, an hour when all decent people slept and nobody was out stirring up something.

"Oh mama," a woman's voice cut through the dark. "It's your sweet baby girl and she's hurting."

Revis stopped. The voice came from his front porch. He tiptoed into the living room. He didn't know why, then he jumped back. Someone stood on his front porch. The shape moved, came toward the door and knocked.

Revis wished he had kept looking for his gun; it was old and rusty and he didn't know if it fired, butthe shape of it might stop somebody. He could say, "Don't come any closer. I've got a gun and I know how to shoot." Which wasn't a lie. He did have a gun. He just didn't happen to have it with him right now. And he did know how to shoot, which he would do if he had his gun and the occasion called for it. He knew he could.

The person knocked again, this time rattling the glass, trying the knob.

Revis held the knob with both hands. It was round and cold as an egg. "What you want?"
"Drink a water," the man said, "that's all."

Ha, Revis thought. You think you got me now. I get you a drink of water and I have to open the door to give it to you and you'll have me then.
"We got somebody out here hurt," the
man said.

"How bad?" Revis asked.

"Not so bad she can't drink water," the man said. "Take something stronger if you got it."

Revis then thought of his homemade wine. Scuppernong. He used it to soak fruitcakes at Christmas. He mixed it with brown sugar to cure a cough. Sometimes he liked a cold glass to sip at the end of the day that couldn't end soon enough. It helped him sleep. In his mind he counted pale blue quart jars on the basement shelf, Four. Maybe only three. He didn't know these people. Maybe homemade wine wasn't strong enough for them. He didn't want to waste it and he didn't want to be laughed at. Somebody might say what he had was just grape juice with an attitude.

Revis counted shapes of three people beside a car in his front yard. The one on the porch made four.

"How'd you get here?" he said through the glass.

"Rode," the man said. "And I'd still be riding if the road hadn't quit on me."

Road didn't quit on you, Revis wanted to say. You just ran off it slap dab in the middle of my yard. Maybe they didn't need anything more to drink than water.

"You got a flashlight?" the man asked.

"Not handy," Revis said.

"How about getting one handy?" The man turned back toward the car. "We don't know who's bleeding and who's not. Who spilled what they were drinking or not."

"I'll call somebody for you," Revis said.

"No, don't want you to do that. You got no cause to go to all that trouble when all we need is a little water and some light."

A moan came from one of the women near the car.

"You wreck?" Revis asked.

"Nawh," the man answered, "car just took a notion to straighten that curve some."

"Stay here," Revis said.

"No place to go." The man put his face to the glass.

Still in the dark, Revis went down the hall and into the kitchen.

There was enough light coming in the window that he took a glass from the shelf and started to fill it under the faucet. Then he took ice. They might need ice, so he reached in the refrigerator and filled the glass with ice. There was a box of frozen peas next to the ice cube bin, so he took those and the glass of water and went out the back door. He always forgot to lock that door. Anybody walking through the night could have come right in, got in his bed and he wouldn't have thought a thing about it until morning.

The grass was silver with dew and looked like a light snowfall. Several times Revis slid a little and the water in the glass sloshed, spilled across his fingers cold as death.

When he came around the house, the man still stood on the porch and the women were huddled around each other by the car, which was bigger and darker than he thought.

He took the water to the women. One of them, the tallest, wore a big hat and held a pocketbook on her arm flat and wide as a package.

"That was kind of you." She took the water, then helped herself to a little sip as if she needed to test it. "Too cold and she might go into shock. Though this ride has been enough of a shock for all of us." She held the glass for the woman who seemed to still be moaning under her breath. "Drink it slow and you'll feel better."

Revis held the box of green peas in a cold spot next to his chest. "I brought these in case there's a swelling. A bruised place. Doctor told me once no use buying a ice pack, when you got a pack of anything in the freezer. Just put that on the place."

The taller woman took the box of peas and turned them over in her hands. "Well, I never," she said.

The woman drinking the water started to laugh. "I never thought when I started to church tonight I'd end up fifty miles from home in a stranger's front yard holding a box of green peas to my head."

The third woman got back in the car. She walked past Revis so close he smelled her perfume. Petunias. She smelled funny and sweet as the petunias Louise used to grow in hanging baskets on the porch. You couldn't walk in the door without hitting one smell that would follow you in the house for fifteen minutes or so. He didn't like it, but he didn't hate it either. "You all come far?"

"Not as far as we're going," the woman said. She jangled a gold bracelet and wore hoops big as doughnuts in her ears. When she opened the car door, he saw she was smiling, wearing a hat too. One with a veil turned up and a red feather like a little wing in one side. Revis was glad he'd put on his shirt. Wouldn't do to be half-naked around people like these even if it was past midnight.

"We like to be on the road when there's not so much passing," the man who'd come up behind Revis said. "Nights like this you can see where you're going as good as if you had street lights."

"Where does this road go?" the woman with the feather in her hat asked.

"Where do you want it to go?" Revis asked. He liked being the one who asked questions.

"Straight up," said the driver. "Straight and narrow and straight up." He almost sang the words to a little tune he hummed. He patted his feet on the grass in Revis's yard, snapped his fingers and laughed. "We are all His children and we gotta make time."

"What kind of car is this?" Revis asked when the woman handed back his glass without so much as a thank you.

He walked toward the rear of the car. The car was some dark color. Black, probably and had fins, like that Buick he owned back in the Fifties. But their fins were wider, stuck out more, like wings. Maybe the car wasn't a car at all but some sort of rocket.

The woman who had bumped her head let the taller woman help her in the backseat and the man who knocked and waited on the porch said, "You reckon we can get started again? I like to get where I'm going before the sun comes up."

He held the car door for the other woman, who got in the front seat. When he shut it and walked around to Revis, he put out his hand. "Mighty obliged, friend. Get in and go with us."

The man's handshake was strong but his hand was soft as a preacher's, open and warm. He held the door to the backseat and Revis hesitated, looked back at the house. There wasn't a light on. Nothing to show anyone lived there. He thought about his homemade scuppernong wine, said, "If you all give me a minute, I'll be right back."

The way back to the house was shorter this time or else his feet moved faster. In the basement he took the jars off the shelf, put them in a half-bushel basket and stuffed newspaper around them. Upstairs, he got his flashlight, change of underwear and three pair of clean socks, then he locked the house, put the key under the doormat and went back to the vehicle. He had been afraid it would be gone or even that it wasn't real ... that he dreamed the whole thing, but no, they were still there. They waited on him.

He got in the backseat beside the woman who held the box of green peas to her forehead. "You were lucky," he said.

"We all were," the man in the front said and started the engine, which gave a steady purr and a small whine as it moved past the maples Revis planted thirty years ago.

They seemed to float above the ground, even rise a little. Revis didn't hear the road beneath them. He saw his neighbor's mercury vapor lights like little dots below him. The ride took his breath away. They rode in the blue-black night. They rode over streets Revis had known all his life, his white steepled church, the red brick bank, the hospital where Louise died, until finally down below there were only fields, a lake, flat and silver as rain.

Going wasn't nearly as bad as he thought.

The Man Who Met a Mermaid Story

Mr. Dewitt Hears the Mermaid

Chalmers Dewitt sat on the edge of his bed and looked at his knotted old feet. He hasn't worn shoes for years, only red felt slippers he could slide. He bet he'd worn out a hundred pair of those slippers the last ten years.

Morning Obituaries "brought to you by Harbinger's Florist Flowers show you care at a time you can share" played on his radio, but above the molasses-voiced announcer, Dewitt heard water running. Water running hard and loud and fast somewhere in his house.

At first he thought it was the kitchen faucet. That it had broken on its own and started pouring a flood. The faucet jerked and sputtered all its life, hung loose from its base.

Dewitt slid to the kitchen, stood hands on the paint-slick doorway and studied. Nothing moved. Nothing in the checkered kitchen stirred a lick. Not even the tired curtains. Nothing but the hands of the electric clock, a black plastic skillet that had a rooster and a hen on top, two fried eggs liked crossed eyes in the middle.

In the quiet kitchen, bacon fat sat cool and tan in the cup on the stove. Drinking glasses were washed and turned upside down on the dishtowel to dry, cabinet doors were shut and still. The faucet wasn't dripping. Water didn't run in this kitchen. Still, he heard water running. Somewhere in his house.

Dewitt eased himself around the corner toward the bathrooms and stopped. The door was closed. He hadn't closed the bathroom door in fifteen years. Not since Elnora died. Nobody here but him and B.C., and B.C. used the bathroom off the back porch when he was here.

Dewitt thought he saw his bathrobe swing on the door hook as if somebody had closed it in a hurry.

"B?" he called. "Buster, that you?"

"It's me," a woman's voice ran above the pounding water. "It's me, O Lord, and the water is hot, hot, hot."

Dewitt dropped his hands from the knob that felt warm and moist. Or was it his hand that was warm and wet?

"Some glad morning," the woman sang in a high, sweet soprano. "When this world is over, I'll fly away."

Dewitt steadied himself and scooted back to his radio. "The deceased is survived by thirteen grandchildren, twenty-seven great grandchildren and six half brothers and sisters." He snapped the radio off, but the singing kept going.

"I'll fly away, O glory," the woman's voice seeped into his room like a stream. "I'll fly away." She turned off the tap and splashed now, hummed and sang. When she dropped something that made a dull thudding sound, she said, "Damn," then splashed and went back to singing. "I'll fly away."

Fly away and she flew here, Dewitt thought. Maybe she'd just fly on out his window. The voice switched to another hymn now. "Love lifted me. When nothing else would do, love lifted me."

Or was Dewitt hearing things?

He eased the door a crack, saw the milky shoulders and back of a woman in his bathtub, a tangle of red hair. She half turned toward him, holding a huge blue sponge over one creamy breast. "Come on in ... help yourself, I don't care." She squeezed the sponge. Water ran down her shoulder in a silver fringe. "When nothing else would do ..."

On the floor lay a big leather pocketbook and beside it a bedspread wrapped in plastic. One of those chenille kind with colored rows and swirls in a pattern. This one looked like a peacock from the colorings, but Dewitt didn't say anything. There was a big straw hat, dusty and wide brimmed, at his feet.

She saw him look at it. "Try it on, hon. Might fit." She giggled. "You never know these things 'til you try."

Dewitt picked up the hat and laid it on his head, where it sat like a platter under a cake. He looked at himself in the medicine cabinet mirror and scratched his cheek. He should have shaved this morning. B.C. got after him about that. Sure as he didn't shave, somebody always came, caught him stubble-faced. Today it was her.

He watched the redheaded woman in the mirror, rubbing and squeezing the sponge all over herself and smiling. Dewitt hadn't seen a woman so naked in all his life. Elnora always kept herself covered up with flannel gowns and knitted underthings and pink panties that hung to her knees. Toward the last he never even saw her knees. This woman hummed and splashed, giggled like she lived here. She acted as if she'd been in this bathroom all her life and he was her husband or something.

"This thing's got feet," she said. Dewitt knew his tub had feet. He'd put this tub in sixty years ago when he bought this country church building and made a house from it. Old bell still stood in the yard, rusty and vine-wrapped. Church was so poor they never had a steeple. Not that they stayed in business long enough to need one. Baptists were always fitting and splitting.

"I never been in one with feet before," she said and cut her blue eyes at him.

Dewitt noticed she had spiky little teeth. A million freckles dusted her face. She wasn't young. No girl had breasts that big and hanging, nipples, dark, round as chocolates. She was thick in her waist, too, and as she bent one knee to wash her thigh, Dewitt saw a wink of red lower hair that was brighter than the mass on her head.

He pulled the hat string tight under his chin and his own face tightened, stared mournfully back at him. He looked like the world's oldest cowboy wearing a too-little hat. He took the hat off and held it somewhere near his heart.

"This tub's so big," she said, picking at a scab on her knee. She smiled at him and he saw a fire behind her eyes like one of those pilot lights in a stove. She lifted her hair with one hand, washed the same shoulder she'd washed only minutes ago.

"Lord, I love a bath," she said. "I could stay in here all day. If somebody would just rent me a bathtub and all the hot water in the world, I'd be happy. Nobody would have to worry about what to do with me then. I'd live in a tub." She kicked and splashed water on him, sprinkled his pants leg.

"My mama always said she'd never seen a child love a bath like I did. How I could be so dirty and clean at the same time."

He stared at the water beading on the floor. Elnora hated this linoleum, green and yellow splatters like confetti. She always said it looked like pond scum. He'd never really looked at it before.

"Honey," the woman said, "if you'll just get me some big bath towels, I'll hop on out of here ... bad as I hate to."

The linen closet smelled of camphor. Everything in it was gray as sage. He pulled out a gray striped towel and handed it to her.

"Lord," she said, "that reminds me of bars. I hope I never see another iron bar on a window in my life."

Window, thought Dewitt. That's how she came in, but none of the windows in the house had been raised in years. None but the one in his bedroom, and that had a screen on it. He'd been sitting right in front of that window when he first heard the water running. How had she gotten in?

He backed from the room as she pulled the plug and he heard water start to drain with a mighty suction. He hadn't used the tub since B.C. had built a shower in the hall with rails to hold stepping in and out.

Dewitt lowered himself into his upholstered rocker and held the straw hat on his lap, waited for the door to open.

She seemed to take forever. He heard her wipe the tub and maybe every surface in the bathroom. The medicine cabinet rattled, glass in the window squeaked, and she even moved the wastebasket and hamper on the floor. Finally she sprayed something, clicked back on a cap. He thought that spraying hiss sounded for all the world like one of those automatic door closers they used to have on the barbershop. He thought he smelled shampoo and lilac and baby powder with a whiff of vanilla. She sang again. "You are my sunshine, my only sunshine. You make me happy when ..."

She did seem happy. What if she decided to stay? There was a whole upstairs: six bedrooms he used to rent to teachers when there was a school in Blue Hill. He still had the living room, even if he couldn't sit in there now without hearing Elnora scold, her voice tinny and rasping as when she'd been alive. Off the living room was Elnora's bedroom, prim and pink- flower patterned as the day she died. Her clothes were flat in the closet, hats on the shelf and covered with plastic (Elnora believed in protecting things), face powders and creams on her dresser. Dewitt liked to show people Elnora's room, pick up her slippers, pink and gold- threaded. He'd left them, like she used to, beside her bed. That impressed people. They'd mumble things, like, "You must have loved her a lot." And he'd nod, sometimes feel his eyes mist up. If he kept at it, his chin quivered a wibble or two.

When the woman came in from the bathroom, she wore jeans, a wrinkled and faded calico blouse. She looked clean. She brushed her hair, leaned to one side as she stroked. "Don't guess you'd have a blow dryer, would you?"

Before he answered, she said, "Well, you can't have everything. You wouldn't believe what some of the places I use have: sun lamps and a little massage unit, whirlpools and little shelves you pull from the wall to prop your feet on to do your nails, towels big and thick enough to die in. One place had heated towels, but I can't go back there. They know me now."

"Who?" he finally said, trying to get out a whole sentence about who are you and how did you get in? "Who ..." he started again.

"Oh, I don't remember who. One of those fancy chains you see advertised on TV a lot. But they charge you an arm and a leg."

She pulled a piece of rope from her pocket and for a moment Dewitt stiffened in his chair. She was going to tie him up and rob him, leave him here. He should have known a strange woman didn't come singing and bathing in your house and leave without something. He thought of the war bonds in his trunk and with a little intake of his breath, heard his own voice go, "Oh."

She tied her hair back with the rope. "I stole this, but you won't tell. Or is it stealing when you find something in a package by the side of the road, brand new, all wet and still in a coil."

She went back to the bathroom for her bag and the spread, came back holding her shoes: thick wooden-soled ones with a wide clear plastic band across the top perforated and studded with sequins.

She sat on his bed, the quilt Elnora had made, unrolled a coil of socks, then rolled them onto her feet, smoothed her instep and ankles and calves like she loved them. She wiggled into her shoes and thumped the floor. "Loud," she laughed then stamped again and twirled, still holding her hairbrush. "I wouldn't be walking if my car hadn't quit." She brushed the red tangles long and out, then back and down, holding lengths of hair and brushing, petting it like a kitten on her chest. "This stuff takes so long to dry. You wouldn't believe how long it takes." She came near him. "Here," she said, "feel. It's still wet."

"How," he began again and stopped, began over and fast, "How did you get in?" She was so close he couldn't breathe ... All that hair in his face, the bulk of her body shutting out the light. He felt he might smother.

"Oh, baby," she said, "is that what's worrying you?" She danced away ... "There's not a house made that don't have some little leak. A crack I can slip through like a snake. Leave a little space for air and I get my hands in, pull the rest of me through.

She turned toward the hall door. "But I never go out the way I came in ... that's bad luck, my mama always said. Or is it the other way?" She twisted her face, wrinkled her nose. "Your upstairs sure is dusty. And those beds. Hard, honey. I've slept in barns and haylofts softer than those. Don't worry," she said flinging her pocketbook strap over her shoulder. "I never come to the same place twice. Not anymore. And I always leave cleaner than I came." She clomped into the hall, gave a flick of a wave, then squeaked and slammed the screen door. A few minutes later he thought he heard the rust- muffled ring from the bell in the yard, but he wasn't sure.

When B.C. came home, he'd want to know about all that water and wet towels. Dewitt picked a red hair off his pants leg and twisted it around his thorny old finger so tight a throbbing pain began.

The Dutiful Daughter's Story

Doing a Demo and the Double-Wide Wedding Dress

"Mama's gone," Clemmie Rink said a million times a day. She said it like a child whose Mama had simply gone to the store and would be back in a few minutes. She said it when she crawled into her mother's bed at night and slept between sheets that smelled of Mama, all tan and wrinkled and yellow. Clemmie said it when she brushed her hair and cleaned the brush of her own long darkness mixed with Mama's white fuzz. She said it when she washed only one plate and glass and fork in the kitchen. Sometimes she said it like a shout. Like someone who had just been released from a locked room.

That last endless night had been three days. Clemmie kept the shade pulled, and each time Mama roused up she'd ask, "Is it morning?"

And Clemmie answered, "Not yet," when it had been morning three times already.

Once, when Mama roused up, she asked Clemmie what made her give that little glass vase to Grace Boney?

"What vase?" Clemmie held the juice glass to her mother's lips, which were pale as light before dawn and veined with blue.

"My little vase," her mother said.

Her mother had a dozen vases, two dozen, three. What was one?

"The milk glass vase you gave Grace Boney," her mother whispered and sank back into her pillow. "You know she never liked me."

"I don't know a thing about a milk glass vase and as for Grace Boney, I haven't seen hide nor hair of her in a thousand years."

"You lie." Her mother spat the words like phlegm.

Clemmie couldn't for the life of her think of a milk glass vase in this house, and she had lived here all her life, all forty-three years. She thought of that horrible orange fluted vase that stood on the corner of the piano in the sitting room, which was named right, because the only thing you ever did in that room was sit. And clean, of course. Dust those damn little China doggies and kitties. Lord help her if she broke a paw or tail off one. And she thought of that squatty pink vase with warts all over it that sat on the sideboard in the dining room. She thought of a crystal vase with a gold medallion on it that had belonged to Grandma and was too precious to even put a peony in.

"What vase?" Clemmie held the empty juice glass, rocked back on her heels.

"My milk glass," Mama said. "Milk glass." She repeated over and over like Clemmie was stupid. "Milk glass."

"You never had a milk glass vase," Clemmie started out. This business was going nowhere and she had things to do. Mama thought this house ran itself. Groceries came in the door, cooked themselves, and the pots and pans cleaned themselves when you turned your back. Ha! She wished.

"She always wanted it." Mama closed her eyes. And before Clemmie could ask who? Who wanted it? Mama said, "Grace Boney never let me have a minute's peace after I won it that Christmas playing Dirty Bingo at the VFW party."

Which must have been a hundred years ago, Clemmie thought. Don't argue with your Mama, Daddy always told her with a finger over his lips. "You don't want to get her blood pressure up." So Clemmie lied and tried to always tell her Mama what she wanted to hear. She agreed with whatever Mama said, even if Clemmie had to cross her fingers behind her back and feel her breath heating up like a teakettle in her chest.

"Mama," Clemmie said, "just rest, will you?" What she wanted to say was let it rest, the whole Grace-Boney-milk-glass-vase subject. Kill it. Bury it. I never want to hear the mess again.

"I don't know why you did it, but I want you to go right this minute and get my vase back." Mama raised a trembling arm, pointed a wickedly long finger and shook it. "Go, I said, go." "You go, Mama," Clemmie said. "I'm not going out of this house at this hour on some crazy business you made up to get back at me for something. I don't know what, but something. It's not enough I've spent my life taking care of you ... my whole life." The empty juice glass slid out of Clemmie's hand and hit the glass dresser top, with a crack that sent a jagged break all the way across, where it popped like a firecracker when it reached the edge.

Mama jumped with a cry like an old buzzard being shot. "My heart." She clutched her chest. "My heart can't stand such as this."

"Your heart's stronger than mine," Clemmie said and slammed the door shut.

Then she stormed from the house and sat in the porch swing that let out a groan when she lowered herself into it. She sat in the dark until sometime in the morning when the house seemed entirely too quiet. She listened. Even the crickets in the yard had hushed.

That was when she went back in and found her mama dead as a rock, her eyes sunk back so far in her head you only saw black holes and the top of her head shiny as the bottom of a pot.

"Ma." Clemmie tiptoed toward her. "Ma, you awake?"

She knew different, but she lifted her mother's hand where it lay atop the cover and stroked the stiff, cool fingers. Then Clemmie let out a howl, a howl so sharp and loud it woke Mayfield Murlow across the street. Mayfield sat bolt upright in bed, clutched the neck of her nightdress and said out loud, "Lord, help us, it's happened. It's happened."

"I knew the minute it happened. Miss Ila's going. Lord help us, I said and sat up in bed. I said to myself, it's happened," Mayfield told Truma Arscott, who had lived next door for the last forty years. "Then a week later she does something like this. First she up and kills her mama, and next thing you know she goes plum crazy and puts that house up for sale. Where in this world does she think she's going to live? Who is going to take her in?"

Truma shook out her gardening gloves, squeezed and pulled each stiff finger like you'd do to get the last dab of toothpaste from the tube. "You never know where those brown recluse spiders might decide to come and hide," she told Mayfield, and she sure didn't want to shove her finger right down into the mouth of one. Why, her cousin Kathleen got bit by one on the elbow and within an hour her whole arm was swollen like an inner tube. They had to take off the whole thing, and the rest of her life she went around with that arm of her dresses and sweaters pinned flat and back behind her. Walked a little sideways too.

"I would hate to see what that house looks like inside," Mayfield said. She wore her straw gardening hat and size 24W paisley printed purple shorts. When she bent over the glare off those winter white thighs almost blinded passersby. That's what Truma said after she told Mayfield she ought to cover herself a little better when she worked in the yard.

"Skin cancer just loves to sneak up on places the sun don't shine. Inside thighs and such. The bad, bad, bad kind. All it takes is one zap and you got it."

Mayfield had never heard such a thing, and she kept on wearing those purple shorts whenever she wanted to.

She knew Truma felt she had done her Christian duty saying that and now she'd shut up after she had warned. She was off the hook should anything happen. "My mother-in-law, God bless her soul, told me when I was a brand-new little, not big as a minute, bride, a lot more people see the outside of your house than would ever see the inside. That's what made me start spending so much time on my yard. Not that it ever shows it, of course." She waited for Truma to correct her. Which she did.

"Why, Mayfield, your yard always looks a picture. I don't know anyone who does so much—"

"And has so little to show for it." Mayfield laughed, waved her hedge clippers. The row of bushes quaked.

All the bright green new growth on the hedge shivered and shook, knew its next hour was all. Then it would be no more than a pile of clippings in the giant compost bin in the backyard.

Mayfield's tulips straightened up, nodded nicely to her. Her jonquils and crocus glistened like smiles. Every one of Mayfield's spring bulbs bloomed where they were planted. They bloomed in perfect rows. They didn't dare do otherwise. She'd lop their heads off without half a thought. "At least," Mayfield said, "my flowers are real. I'd never stoop to silk in my yard in a million years. A trillion years."

Truma clucked her tongue as both of them stared across the street. "Tacky, tacky."

Which was the very word Mayfield started to say. "If that child wanted to put clusters of yellow jonquils up and down the driveway for a few weeks ... while the real ones are blooming ... and then take them up when the season's over, why nobody would think a thing about it. Jonquils look real. I've never seen a silk rose that did. And even if they did, they wouldn't grow in clumps like she put out. Blue? Orange? They look like something you'd put on a grave."

"Maybe she's making up for the flowers she didn't put on her mama's grave," Truma snorted and bent to pull up a stalk of wild onion. She tugged and tugged but the onion hung on like its roots looped all the way to China and back. "You know how she couldn't wait to get that woman in the ground. Died one day, buried the next. And not much of a funeral to speak of. Didn't even call the preacher until it was all over. Said he didn't come around before, why should she call him now?" Truma gave the onion a quick hard jerk that broke it off even with the ground and landed her hard on her haunches. Whump! Her breath came out in one round sound.

"Don't it make you wonder," Mayfield whacked the hedge, stopped and looked skyward, "exactly where that woman is right now? She never bothered to darken the door of a church when she was alive." Mayfield shaded her eyes with one hand. "Not that I ever saw."

"Me neither," Truma said, hauled herself up and looked skyward too. She focused on the same big bag of cotton puffy clouds that were spilled across the sky.

"This child is going to need some help. Between you and me, it will take pro-fess-ional help to get her back on the road."

"What road?" Truma glanced up and down the street.

"The road to doing something with her life, little that it is." Mayfield piled hedge clippings in her wheelbarrow.

"She sat in the ditch too long. That morning all she would say is 'Mama's gone, Mama's gone. Flew the coop. Up and left, hit the road.' She raised both arms in the air and just sat there."

"She's always been a strange one," Truma said. She aimed her hoe at a dandelion, stepped back and cut its head off.

"There she sat," Mayfield said, "helpless as a baby, big as she is, and crying her head off. I rushed over but she wouldn't talk to me. Wouldn't answer a thing I said. 'Honey, I said, 'Help yourself up.' I held out my arm and said, 'Grab ahold of me and pull.' But she wouldn't do it. Kept sitting there saying I never told her goodnight. All my life, I kissed my Mama good night. I couldn't sleep until I told her I loved her and kissed her. And now Mama's gone.' Clemmie just sat in the ditch hugging her knees and rocking herself. I was the one to call the undertaker and then she wouldn't let me in the house. So I sat on the porch until he came. Then I left her to go about her business, thinking she'd need me later. Later never came. Even at the funeral she sat by herself and never shed a tear.

"'When Mama was alive,' Clemmie said, 'I cooked what she said and we ate what she wanted, when she wanted. If she wanted candied yams at midnight, I made them. If she wanted cheese grits for a bedtime snack, I stirred them up, made red-eye gravy to go with them. Whatever Mama wanted. Now I eat steak three times a day if I feel like it. One morning all I wanted for breakfast was watermelon, so that's what I had. Best breakfast I ever ate. Mama always had to have her ham and eggs. Now I'm selling the stove I cooked on and the table we ate on until Mama got too sick to come to the kitchen. I'm selling the chairs we sat on and the bed she slept in. I'm selling the porch swing and Grandma's quilts. Old smelly musty things. I'm selling everything but the dust in the chest of drawers in this house. And people are buying. People will buy anything. Even Grace Boney came looking to buy another milk glass vase to match the one mama gave her. Gave her, mind you. Mama herself and she accused me. When Grace Boney said that I said, 'Would you mind repeating what you just said and saying it a little louder?' I wanted to be sure Mama heard. I know she's hiding around here till I get things straightened out, then I'll have to go and find her. She likes to hide, make me call and call, look in every closet and crawl space. But I know what she's aiming to do and we'll meet there. She won't be a bit surprised. Just say, 'What took you so long? I thought you'd never get here.'"

Mayfield and Truma watched now from inside Mayfield's living room. Each had a window. Each stood slightly to one side and pulled back the drapery just a little to get a better view. They watched pickup trucks load Miss Illa's dining room table with twelve matching chairs. The upholstered cushions had been burgundy once. Now they were a muted red. "Wonder what she got for that?" Mayfield said. "It wasn't cherry, just some dark finish. I doubt it was even solid wood. Of course I only saw it once and that's been years ago."

"Has the child got anything left to sit on?" asked Truma.

They watched people carry unassembled beds to assorted trucks and trailers. Dressers, footstools, end tables, lamps. They saw Grace Boney walk out with a rolled-up throw rug under her arm. "Grace Boney," both of them mouthed to each other.

"She hadn't been in that house in a hundred years, I bet. Not since she and Illa had words over some bingo prize."

"Is she getting rid of everything?" Truma asked. "What's she going to do? Sleep on the floor?"

"She's lost her mind."

"We have every right to go in that house," Truma said. "We can be customers too. I might see that glass basket that got missing from my house once upon a time. It went somewhere and I've never thought it went far."

"Who's to say we're not customers?" Mayfield dropped her handful of drapery. "Our money's the same color as anybody else. And probably a whole lot cleaner."

"I don't know many people who wash every bill that comes in their house like you do." Truma followed Mayfield to the kitchen. "Soap and water, then iron them dry."

"I've always said as many people who have their hands-on money and you don't know where those hands have been before, we'd all be a whole lot healthier if everybody washed their money." Mayfield took bread from her refrigerator, mayonnaise. "Let's take Clemmie a little lunch. She's got to be hungry." She handed Truma a can of tuna to open. "I mix in a little onion if I have it. If I don't, I do without." She didn't get Truma an onion.

Truma mixed in pickles. "I like mustard in mine."

"I never heard such a thing." Mayfield laid flat two slices of bread. "Don't you put mustard anywhere near me. I've never been able to tolerate the stuff. My stomach's much too sensitive." She wrapped the sandwich with crisp waxed paper, creased sharp corners, then taped down the two ends. Then she patted the sandwich for being obedient, like a good child.

"I bet Frank Upchurch has the dirtiest money in town," Truma said as they crossed the street.

"Really dirty or just how he made it?" Mayfield asked.

"Both." Truma held her lips tight together. "I wouldn't be a bit surprised if the sheriff arrested him tomorrow."

"You heard something!" Mayfield stopped in the middle of the street, put her hand on Truma's arm.

"I don't have to," Truma said.

Mayfield let go and they both started down the driveway Clemmie had lined with every color and size and shape of silk flower the Dollar Store had in stock. When they passed the For Sale sign and the Tag Sale sign, both women looked the other way. Neither sign was something they wanted to see.

They passed people carrying stacked high loads of bedspreads, sheets, towels, pillows. One had a canary cage on top of his stack. Another, a potted plant, tall and prickly as a cactus. The plant wore a child's red cowboy hat. And a smile. "If she sells Miss Lula's and Miss Illa's quilts, she'll be sorry. Nobody will pay what they're worth ... and they are worth hundreds, hundreds," Mayfield said. "Or will be in a few years."

"They kept scraps from half the country," Truma said. "Miss Lula sewed for the public, taught Miss Illa and I heard tell both of them kept scraps from every garment they made for anybody. The whole town is in those quilts."

"Clemmie," Mayfield called from the porch after she knocked on the door and there was no answer. "For all we know," she said to Truma, "she's sold every knife and fork in the place and is just sitting over here half starved."

Truma, who couldn't imagine Clemmie half hungry, much less half starved, called into the darkness, "Clemmie, honey, it's us."

Boxes were stacked waist high on the porch. Truma peered into one. "Looks like dishes," she said and picked up an oval platter with a turkey painted in the center.

"Nothing matches. Odds and ends, I guess. We all have to clean out our cabinets sometime in our life. I dread just thinking of mine."

They heard thumps, several bumps and some shuffling noises from upstairs. They called Clemmie again. The only answer was another thump.

They looked at each other. "You think she's all right?"

Truma held open the screen door and Mayfield went in first. Both tiptoed. There were round spots on the wallpaper where pictures and mirrors had hung. On the floor were dark, squared areas where rugs had been taken up.

In the corner of the living room was a rocking chair with a sign hung on its chest: "Not For Sale at Any Price. Don't Ask." An afghan with a jagged tea stain lay draped across one arm. Or was it a pee stain? Truma pointed it out to Mayfield.

"I'd get rid of that thing, no matter what made that stain." A guitar with a broken string on its lap looking like a mahogany child.

"Some stuff you can't give away. You just toss and forget it," Mayfield said.

"Clemmie," Truma called.

At the top of the stairs, bright eyes looked down behind hair that hung long and loose over the rail. "Here," Clemmie called, "I'm up here."

"Well come down, sweetie. We brought you a little bite of lunch," Mayfield called. She held the paper bag by its neck.

"Leave it in the kitchen," Clemmie said. "I'll eat later."

"It's after two," Truma said. "You need something."

"We put in oatmeal cookies," Mayfield sang. "The kind with raisins. You need strength."

"I need to get this house emptied out," Clemmie said.

Truma and Mayfield crept up the stairs.

"Nails," said Mayfield. "Where those pictures hung. I use those things you drive in sideways and they don't leave holes."

At the top of the stairs, a mattress stood on its end. There was a rusted trunk and a coffee table with a broken leg. Hanging from the facing over a door swung a huge white dress. It flapped Mayfield and Trauma as they walked by.

"Lord," Mayfield said, "what in the world is that thing?"

The dress had long sleeves and a row of little buttons from the high neck all the way to the hem. It was as wide as the open doorway and then some.

"It's my mama's wedding dress." Clemmie came from the room behind it. "And it's not for sale."

Mayfield turned to Truma and both of them mouthed who-would-buy-such-a-thing-in-the-first-place? to each other.

"Grandma Lula made it. Raw silk." She rubbed the nubs. "Mama wanted to be buried in it, but it was five times too big. She always called it her doublewide wedding dress. And I reckon it is." Clemmie took the dress down and hugged it close. "When she and my daddy got married, they lived in a trailer in Texas. Till she came home to have me and never went back. Who would? Texas in the summer time? They parted, Mama said, and stayed parted. He never saw me." Clemmie folded the dress in half, then half again, like a tent. "Never even saw my picture."

Mayfield fingered the dress draped over Clemmie's arm. Might be called silk. Sure didn't feel like any silk she'd ever felt. And not something anybody with taste would be caught dead in, much less married.

"So that's what give me the idea," Clemmie went on, still holding the dress. "Me and Mama's gonna live in a double wide in a trailer park near Graceland. That's where she is now. She's waiting for me."

"Honey." Truma reached to pat Clemmie's arm, but Clemmie stepped back so Truma ended up with her hand stopped in midair.

"Your mama's buried," Mayfield said. "She died in this house. Don't you remember? You screamed and ran out the door and I called 911 and they came and got your Mama."

"That was pretend. She hides all over this house and I have to find her. That's when I got the idea of Graceland. Only she up and went first."

"You need to eat something," Mayfield said. "It's hot up here. Hot and dusty and you need nourishment." She started toward Clemmie.

Clemmie held the dress and backed away. "Raccoons." She pointed her finger at both of them and shook it hard. "You are raccoons from Hell. Both of you."

The women gasped, put their hands over their hearts and looked at each other. Mayfield dropped the lunch bag, took Truma's arm and pulled her down the hall and down the steps, jerked her hard and fast. Truma stopped halfway, said, "Lord, let me catch my breath a minute."

"I don't believe she said that."

"Said what?"

"Never mind," said Mayfield, pulling Truma out the front door and past a young couple coming in. The girl wore a pink halter-top and rolled up jean shorts. She was barefooted, had polished her toenails black and had a ring with a big green stone in her navel. The boy had a ring in his nose and black hair that waved to his waist. His t-shirt read, "Born to Raise Hell." He raised one arm to the women. "Hidy," he said. "I'm Roy Boy and this is Darnelle, my little darling for the time being. We just bought this place and we're fixing to move in soon as the fat lady gets her pitiful mess and big ass out." He bent over to light a cigarette, sucked hard on it, and then handed it to the girl.

Mayfield sailed right on by. Truma in tow.

"I heard that," Truma said. "He said they bought this house."

"Didn't you learn a long time ago not to believe everything you hear?" Mayfield sped up the driveway, past the carnival of flowers, past several people tying furniture to their trucks. The people nodded to the women as they passed by. The flowers nodded in the breeze made by those fast walking, furious feet.

Only when they were safe across the street did Mayfield drop Truma's arm. When they got in her living room, she shut the door behind them and said, "I don't know what's going on over there and I don't want to know. I'm going to pretend there's a bare spot where that house used to be, and let's not even talk about it."

"All right," said Truma. "If that's what you want."

It wasn't, but Mayfield felt it was best until the next morning when she saw the recreation vehicle pull in Clemmie's driveway. "It looks like a bus," she hissed to Truma. "A big, beige and white bus. What's she going to do with the thing?"

Clemmie hollered and motioned over the two women, who couldn't get there fast enough. "It's got a refrigerator," she said, and a john and little table that lets down so you can eat and watch TV at the same time. And you could do that all the time if you had somebody to do the driving."

"You be careful, Clemmie," Mayfield said. "A woman alone out on the road can get herself in trouble before she knows it."

"I won't be alone," Clemmie said and led them back to the bed part, where a black and white cat lay round as a cushion. "This is my attack cat," Clemmie said. She pointed to a sticker with those words and a drawing of an angry cat in her back window.

The cat yawned, stretched out a paw, and licked it.

Mayfield saw the cat had no claws. "Honey," she told Clemmie, "I don't know where you got that cat, but if I were you I wouldn't depend on it in a tight spot."

"I don't plan to get in any tight spots. And I got the cat from Grace Boney," said Clemmie. "She gave it to me 'cause I gave her Mama's other little milk glass vase." Clemmie giggled. "I found it in the basement so covered with dust I thought it was black. Washed that vase up and the milk glass was shiny white.

I guess Mama knew what she had and didn't have."

Clemmie shut the door to her RV, locked it, and put the key in her pocket. "I'm hitting the road before daylight tomorrow morning. Tonight's my last night in my girlhood." She sighed. "Graceland, here I come." Mayfield let her breath escape in one long,
loud sigh. "Clemmie, you write us and promise you won't pick up any riders on the road."

"I don't make promises," Clemmie said. "And I got more sense that you ever gave me credit. A thousand times more."

That fall Mayfield let her hedge grow taller, tall as trees, just pruned the sides so nobody could say she was letting things go to rack and ruin. Not that she ever would.

The people who moved into Miss Illa's house did let it go to rack and ruin; they took the screens off the windows, broke off the porch rail, painted every plank a different color and strung little lights shaped like red peppers up and down the eaves.

"And it's not even Christmas," Truma said. "I thought Clemmie was tacky, but these people invented the word."

Right after Halloween, Truma got a card from Clemmie.

She had drawn a pumpkin with a smiley face, a turkey and ghost across the top and around, then wrote, "Having a wonderful time, me and my cat. Haven't seen Elvis yet, but I know he's here. Mama too. Regards, Clemmie."

"Regards!" Mayfield said when she saw the card. "Where did Clemmie ever learn a word like that? Regards what?"

Truma stuck the card on her refrigerator and went back to watching the people in Clemmie's house. It was a full-time job.

They had cars and trucks in and out their driveway all hours of the day and night. The police were there at least once a week, but Mayfield said they came as customers, not because they were called. Though neighbors did call. And complain about the noise, the traffic, the type of people who hung around that house.

Then the day after Thanksgiving, Mayfield and Truma woke up to quiet. Truma knocked on Mayfield's backdoor, still in her robe and slippers. "Do you see what I see?" she said.

"What?" Mayfield listened to her coffee pot drip. She didn't want to think until she'd had her first cup.

"Miss Illa's house is empty as the day Clemmie up and left it."

"Empty?" Mayfield went to her living room window, eased back the curtain.

The house sat as though slumped over, beaten, worn and tired. It sagged from roof peak to porch floor. It was empty.

"Reckon where they went?" Truma said.

"Wherever it was can't be far enough to suit me," Mayfield said. "Just so they don't find their way back."

The house stayed empty. When it snowed in early December, snow stayed on the roof long after every other roof in the neighborhood melted clean. Leaves had blown on the porch and piled into peaks like little brown mountains.

Parts of things, bicycles and motorcycles and ragged ends of carpet, broken bits of plastic toys lay scattered in the yard. The silk flowers Clemmie planted by the driveway had long ago been uprooted by the wind, faded whites and dirty grays, blown next to the house, caught in shrubbery like rags.

"Eyesore," Mayfield said.

"I thought you were pretending it wasn't there," Truma said.

"I am," Mayfield said, with a little paintbrush in her hand as she dusted off her ivory and gold front door Christmas wreath.

At Christmas, when Truma got another card from Clemmie, she brought it over to show Mayfield, who said she didn't even want to see it. "She says she and Mama are doing fine." Truman read, "They cut a demo for us to listen for on the radio. It's called 'Who Wears the Double Wide Wedding Dress?' Why, they may be the next Judds." Truma clasped the card with both hands and held it over her heart.

Mayfield snorted, "You won't catch me listening to any such song if a radio station was fool enough to play it. Judds, my eyes. Rinky Dinks is more like it."

"I wonder if Clemmie has thought of that," Truma asked. "I could just write and tell her."

"You'll do no such thing," Mayfield said, "not and put my name on it."

"I'll put mine," Truma said. And did. But that was the last she ever heard about the new Judds or the Rinky Dinks, which she thought had a musical sound on its own and ought to do something. Not that Clemmie would know and do. The child didn't live in this world. Truma didn't know what world she lived in. In fact, she didn't know what world anybody lived in these days. A demo! Such unexpected things happened. Happened all over the place.

The School Secretary's Story

Friendly Breathing

The green suit was beautiful and it fit perfectly. Amazing, Marianne thought. And it was on sale at a give-away price. "I can't believe this," she said out loud, holding the tag, still looking at herself in the mirror. She always had to have things altered: sleeves, hems, pant legs. There had to be something wrong. Not only did this suit fit, but she didn't have to think twice about the price.

"You're nuts," Alice said. "Buy it. You don't look a gift horse in the mouth. This is a consignment shop, not Montaldo's, for gosh sakes."

The price was almost a gift. But then prices at the consignment shops were the reason you went there. That's what Alice said. Marianne went along because she was with Alice and she was curious.

It was a Saturday. They'd had a nice lunch. Neither of them had to be anywhere at a specific time, so they browsed. And in browsing came to "Nice Twice." Marianne hesitated to go in. The window seemed a jumble of things: women's dresses, a bridal gown, and children's clothes, none of them really nice, a few toys, a silver tea set that had never seen polish.

The "Nice Twice" shop was last in a line of small shops in an older strip shopping center where all the stores had wide expanses of plate glass. Even the glass at "Nice Twice" seemed slightly smudged, as though it had been worn by so many different businesses moving in and out.

"Is this price correct?" Marianne asked the little flip of a dark-haired girl at the cash register who took the tag in her hand and looked it over.

"That's my mom's seven. I'd know it anywhere. Gotta be right." She chewed gum, blew a blue bubble that broke over her nose. She licked it back in. "Want me to ring it up?"

Marianne looked back at Alice, who wore a lace nightgown over her dress. The gown was see through, with long sleeves and thin blue ribbons tied in bows at the neck and wrists. It looked as if it might have been part of a trousseau.

Alice twirled. "I don't have anybody to wear this for, but I'm somebody, aren't I? I'll wear it for me."

"Gus is nobody?" Marianne said.

"Nobody much," Alice said and raised her eyes to the ceiling. "Nobody who counts." She laughed, took the gown off and folded it across her arm, went to the register. "New," Alice said. "Never worn. There's a story here."

The girl blew another bubble. "You sound as daffy as my mom. She'd rather play with this old stuff than go to the mall. I think she's nuts." The girl twirled a finger and pointed to the side of her head. "I been telling her that for years."

Marianne paid for her suit, feeling slightly guilty, as if she should have given them at least a hundred dollars more. It was a designer suit.

"So?" Alice laughed. "You want to pay more, I'm sure they'd let you." They left the shop. "I can't believe I got that gorgeous gown for almost nothing. And it's new."

Monday Marianne wore the suit to school. All day everyone passing through the principal's office commented how nice she looked. Even her principal, Mr. Riddle, nodded after one of the teachers had said what a great suit she was wearing. Usually no one noticed Marianne.

Especially Mr. Riddle. She was a machine he operated by voice command. "Mrs. Bright-Newsome, call central office and tell them the Tuesday afternoon meeting is scheduled at the same time as the district day for all principals and they need to reschedule." Or "Mrs. Bright-Newsom, type a memo to maintenance. There's a drip in my bathroom faucet." Or "Mrs. Bright-Newsom, the end of the month report will have to be redone. I've changed figures on the equipment list."

Sometimes she heard him in her sleep, but then he whispered, his voice husky and low, things like, "Your hair smells delicious. Like apple pie made with Granny Smith apples."

Her hair didn't, of course. Her hair smelled like Breck's, the shampoo she'd used all her life. Some people tried every new brand that came on the market. Not Marianne. She found one and struck to it. Same way with hairstyles, blow dry and brush smooth, flip under, have it trimmed every six weeks.

When she found the notice that central office was hiring for administrative secretary, her first thought was Mr. Riddle. Did she really want to work where she wouldn't see him five days a week? Her next thought, who put the notice in her box? Marianne looked to see if the same blue paper curled in every box. Only hers. Then her next thought, Could she get the job? Twelve years in the system ought to count for something, never missing a day except when Ray died. Then only three. Her job saved her after that. Except for holidays, and then she met Alice at the library discussion group. Big boned and loud, Alice marched to a bass drum in her own oompah band. She and Alice did things on weekends and holidays. Sometimes Marianne's ideas, sometimes Alice's. They got along even if Alice did have Gus, who was gloomy as his name. As long as he had a beer in one hand, TV clicker in the other and some sport on TV, Gus eased through nights and weekends. Marianne and Alice liked plays and movies, shopping.

"Going out for a little retail therapy, girls?" Gus called as he waved them out the door.

Alice's Gus was like a tuba in that oompah band, while Marianne liked to think of herself as a string instrument. Something like a Celtic harp, delicate and plaintive, a high melody that wafted through days and lives and lit on the heads of little children where it played like songs.

She wrote her letter inquiring about the job and listing her qualifications.

That was early October. Still November, when she hadn't heard anything, Marianne wasn't concerned. The wheels in education turned exceedingly slow. Sometimes, just before she went to sleep at night, Marianne pictured herself in her own office on one of the upper floors of an administration building and someone high in the system introducing her as their "right hand." She'd wear sleek suits and bright scarfs and walk briskly down long halls in elegant shoes. She went to sleep smiling and dreamed good things: of trips abroad, ceremonial meals in castles, walking in fragrant English gardens, touring temples in Japan.

When Marianne needed something to wear to the annual Christmas brunch, she tried several chain stores and found nothing. Dresses were too frothy or too sequined, too formal or too short. Her legs weren't bad, but she didn't want to look ridiculous. Not at her age. She even considered the green suit. After all, it was green. But not a Christmas green and besides, she'd worn it so much after fall, everyone had seen it and her in it until she sometimes felt that suit was a second skin. In fact, one of the teachers came up behind her in the cafeteria, tapped her on her shoulder and said, "I need Mr. Riddle's signature on this permit, but yours will do."

"How did you know it was me?" Marianne asked as she handed back the pen.

"I'd know that suit anywhere," the teacher said.

Ouch, Marianne thought, time to give it a bit of a rest, though the suit wasn't showing wear. It was even washable and came out of the dryer each time looking fresh and almost new. Amazing, she thought and tried to read the faded fiber content tag.

So, she called Alice. "Want to go back to that little consignment shop with me?"

Alice had promised to go out of town to a cat show with Lu at two and wouldn't get back before the store closed. "Check the lingerie for me, though, will you?" she asked. "I love that gown I got. See if there's anything else from that number."

"What number?" Marianne asked.

"Every tag has a number code on it. Tells who brought it in."

"Oh," Marianne said.

"I copied the number on my tag so I could remember. It's 647."

Marianne wrote it down. If everything has a number of the person who brought it in, that meant her green suit possibly had sister suits and a dress from the same person's closet. And if the green suit fit so well, maybe other things would too. Worth a try.

There were no other shoppers in the "Nice Twice" shop, and the teenage girl who had been behind the counter the first time had been replaced by a woman with big hair, not big, big hair but tall yellow curls sculpted in large scallops and held in place with a net. She wore earrings that dangled to her neck, a purple tee shirt and skintight jeans with a gold and multi-color jeweled belt. Lord, the woman should be old enough to know better, Marianne thought.

Marianne browsed among the "better dresses"... that's what department stores called their special selection. And to show the dresses were better, they were hung on the rack in plastic bags. "Nice Twice" had followed suit.

Even through the plastic bags, Marianne saw nothing she was interested in and didn't bother to look at numbers on the tags.

Except in the lingerie. There was a blue quilted robe that looked new and had Alice's #647 on it. Marianne left it at the counter, where the woman pricing a stack of clothes glanced up, smiled and said, "You wouldn't think there was this much work running one of these shops. Little did I know."

Next Marianne checked the not-so-dressy dresses. She wanted something classic. Something that wasn't festive, but more than ordinary. She'd know when she saw it. Nothing on the rack. She wished she knew the number of her green suit's original owner.

She asked the woman at the counter and she smiled and shook her head. "Oh, I get asked that all the time, but it's confidential. We can never give out the names of our customers."

"I don't want the name," Marianne said. "Just the number."

"There's no way I can look it up." The woman glanced at a spiral ledger near the telephone. "You'd be surprised at the people who want to know who these clothes belonged to. Why, if we gave out that information, we wouldn't have a business."

Marianne went back to browsing. Near the back wall was a rack marked 50% off. On the rack hung skirts and blouses, slacks with a few dresses at the end. Marianne thumbed through, feeling more discouraged as she neared the end of the rack. Then she saw it. A black jacket dress. She checked the size. Her size! She felt the fabric between her fingers, a twill that was neither glossy nor sleek. Just expensive looking. The jacket had a turned-up collar and three-quarter sleeve, while the dress was plain, but fitted. Oh, if only it would fit.

She took it to the dressing room, slipped off her clothes and into the dress. It zipped easily up the back. She didn't turn to the mirror until she'd put on the jacket. Even before turning around, she knew the fit was perfect and the dress felt as if it had been custom made for her. The number on the tag was 2307. Remember that, she told herself, 2307. And half the already low price. Why had she ever doubted she'd find something here?

At the counter, the woman snipped off the tag but Marianne already had the number 2307. "I've got the perfect pin and earrings for this," the woman said. She pulled a box from beneath the counter. "These just came in." She held the pin to the left side of the jacket. "Now tell me if that isn't the finishing touch."

Marianne agreed, waited for the price on these to be so much it outweighed what she'd saved on the dress. She reached for the pin and earring set, read the price, said, "Great," and saw the number 2307. Whoever owned the black dress also owned the pin and earrings? She left feeling like a thief, the pin and earrings neatly wrapped in tissue and tucked in the bag with the dress. And the woman even said she'd hold the robe for Alice until next week.

"You got the number?" Alice said.

"First thing," Marianne said. "And the best buy on the dress that fits like a dream."

When Marianne described the robe, it sounded too much like one Alice already had, so she called "Nice Twice" on Monday to have it taken off hold.

Marianne's black dress turned out to be stunning. It brought out her even hips, accentuated her breasts and looked just dressy enough. Mr. Riddle even asked her to dance. She thought he smelled like cedars in snow with a hint of heating cinnamon.

She wore the black dress with blouses and turtlenecks through January and every time she wore it, someone always commented, "Nice dress. New?"

"Thank you," Marianne said, "I love wearing it."

It was February before she went back to the "Twice Nice" shop and again without Alice, who said she bet anything Marianne's green suit and black dress had been owned by the same person. Sometimes Marianne tried to imagine that person. She was her age, but lived in a house, not an apartment, across from two old maid sisters who owned the building and tapped on your door at 2 am to use your phone. They called their other sister who lived across town. Insomnia ran in the Booth family and didn't tie up the lines. Marianne had let them in and gone back to sleep more times than she could count. She'd asked once why they didn't have their own phone. They said they worried that a telephone in the house would draw lightning or cause cancer ... She couldn't remember which.

Miss Emily and Miss Addie were like spirits in the night who slipped easily as air out of her apartment, and carefully locked the door behind them. Marianne wondered what they said to their sister in these early hours. Their voices always sounded hushed, soothing, as soft and gray as their faded voile dresses still lightly printed with ghosts of the original pattern, trimmed with mended tatted lace.

"So kind of you, dear," they always said to Marianne. "It's not the expense with us, you understand?" they said in regards to the telephone. "It's the danger. One shouldn't take chances where one's health is concerned," Miss Emily said one night.

Oops, Marianne thought, what if the person whose black dress and green suit she owned had died? Died of some horrible disease. Some contagious disease.

She didn't sleep much the rest of the night and felt as though she moved in slow motion all morning. She certainly didn't sound her usual perky self when the call came from the central office. Could they schedule for an interview?

"Next Thursday," she said, thinking that would give her some time to find something to wear and to prepare.

She'd get Alice to practice interviewing her so she wouldn't be nervous. This was the only job she'd ever been interviewed for and that was so long ago. She'd get letters of recommendation too. If she could get them without Mr. Riddle finding out.

Mr. Riddle, how would he feel about her leaving? She hung up the phone and glanced through the glass at his office. Here she was thinking of leaving and she hadn't gotten the promotion yet.

That night she either dreamed Miss Emily came and whispered in her ear, "You're our sister too. We'll call you," or Miss Emily actually stood by her bed breathing ever so faintly, ever so friendly, patted Marianne's hand with her cool, dry one. Marianne awoke with a start, thought she heard her front door click. But she wasn't sure.

The next morning Alice couldn't go with her to the consignment shop, so Marianne went alone.

This time an older woman sat at the desk reading a thick paperback that she rolled with her hands as she read. She didn't look up when Marianne came in.

What Marianne wanted was another suit. Something smart and classy looking that fitted her to a T. Something that had the same number as the black dress. There was nothing. No suit nor dress nor skirt. Nothing. She looked at numbers *for* numbers. Nothing in all three categories.

"Can you check something for me?" Marianne asked the woman at the desk who glanced up with watery blue eyes. Her glasses slid off her nose, hung by a tiny chain.

"Maybe," the woman said. She looked vaguely familiar.

"Has number 2307 brought anything in lately?"

The woman reached for the notebook and thumbed the pages. Her nails were the color of the underside of a mushroom and had tiny constellations set with stones that winked as her fingers moved.

"Number 2307," Marianne repeated.

"Nothing," the woman said.

"Thanks," said Marianne. "I'll come back again."

That left her exactly where she started, with nothing to wear for the interview. Except the green suit, which she hadn't worn in a while.

She pulled it out of the closet, held it up and said, "Old friend, looks like you're it." She did have it professionally pressed so it would look fresh. Not new. She didn't want to look as if she'd bought something especially for the interview. She wanted something she felt confident in. And comfortable. Plus, she had the perfect scarf for this suit. One that had been in her closet for years. Funny how things almost leapt into your hands at times. She'd felt the green suit did that.

Marianne's interview went so well she couldn't believe it. She was only a tad nervous and soon got over that. She was not unknown in the system. Her work had been noticed. In fact, one of the committee members hinted Marianne had been recruited for the job. She smiled easily, laughed at all the right places, said all the right things. She could tell because members of the interviewing committee nodded their heads, leaned back in their chairs with their arms behind their heads. They couldn't have been more at ease with her.

When they named the salary figure, Marianne felt she reacted like that was exactly what she'd expected when actually it was twice what she'd thought it would be. She caught herself before she said wow. She felt her green suit rein her in just in time. She hesitated only long enough for them to up the salary figure another thousand and promise, in writing, a review with the definite possibility of a raise in three months. Could she let them know her decision within the next week?

She certainly could. Though she knew right now her decision was yes.

"Yes," she told Alice on the phone, "I got the job."

"You're on your way, hon," Alice said. "There's no stopping you now." And Marianne heard Gus in the background say, "A little retail therapy never hurt anybody, I always said."

Marianne did take the job and walk the polished halls in sleek suits and elegant shoes with clicking heels. She got a raise in three months, another in six. She began to buy clothes at the better shops.

Mr. Riddle became Donald, and they went out at least once a week. Sometimes he wanted to sleep over, but Marianne was afraid that would be one of the nights the sisters came to use the phone. He always left before two.

One day she shifted some of her things to the back of the closet to make room for his. The green suit was among them, and the smart little black jacket dress. She held both outfits up a moment longer than the other things before she buried them in the closet.

The next summer, she cleaned that closet. She didn't want to run a newspaper ad to sell the clothes, so she took them to the consignment shop.

"Nice Twice" was still there and the original owner at the desk. The woman with the modified blond beehive reminded Marianne of someone. She couldn't think who. Was she the daughter of the older woman who had looked up numbers for Marianne? Was she the mother of the dark-haired flip of a girl who'd been here when Marianne bought the green suit?

"I usually only take things on Mondays and Tuesdays," the woman said.

"I've never brought anything in before," Marianne said. "And I really can't come back Monday or Tuesday."

"Just leave them," the woman said. "I'll just work them up Monday." She got out her notebook, listed the clothes Marianne had brought. The good old green suit among them.

Marianne wondered if the woman would recognize it. Maybe they wouldn't want something nice thrice. She didn't say anything.

The woman handed her a card. "This is your number. We'll use it for anything you bring in."

Marianne looked at her number. She didn't know what to say. "Does everybody have a different number?"

"They have to," the woman said as she wrote out tags. "No one else is assigned your number." Her voice sounded familiar. Marianne wished she had the nerve to ask the woman to whisper something because she realized who she looked like. The woman looked like Miss Addie and Miss Emily. Same eyes, same shaped face, blonde hair going gray.

"Not ever?" Marianne asked.

"You have the one and only."

"Has anyone else ever *had* this number?"

"Not at this shop." The woman sounded impatient now. "Is there anything wrong with your number? You superstitious or something? I mean some people go crazy if they get near a thirteen."

"No, I'm not superstitious. It's just ..."

"Take it or leave it." The woman closed her book. "I can't sit here and let you pick out the number you want. You gotta take the next one and move on, honey. This is a business."

Marianne sat in her car and held her ticket with the number 2307 for a long time. Long after the woman locked the doors of "Nice Twice" and left. She waved to Marianne, got in her blue Cadillac and backed out, but not before Marianne saw the painting on the car's hood: the painting in whites and golds of a smiling Jesus with his arms outstretched and cartoon balloon form her bearded mouth saying "Come Unto Me." Marianne waited for the next step.

The Family's Story

Joking

My family doesn't tell stories when they get together. They tell jokes. This, though, is a story about my Uncle Drum and Aunt Lillian. Here are two jokes they told. But first we are in the cemetery and birds sing in the tall grass.

Uncle Drum holds the box of ashes close to his chest as though he doesn't want to let it go. I wonder if he hears the birds. If he hears the same song I hear.

The brown and yellow birds flit from tombstone to grass and back again.

"Killdeer," they cry. "Killdeer." And I think how ironic. The birds say what happened.

Now is the time to tell this: how my uncle, a sweet and patient man, killed his wife.

The last time I saw Uncle Drum, here's the joke he told. Two women met in Heaven and started comparing. The food is wonderful, they said. The shopping is absolutely marvelous, the houses are grander than they thought and the men, the men are better than they ever dreamed, one woman confesses. If they'd had any idea it was going to be this good, they would never have eaten all that oat bran.

This was his joke. Aunt Lillian's joke, before the accident was this: a woman dieted all her life. As she left a bridge party, she was hit and killed by an eighteen-wheeler. Two friends saw it happen and said, "I bet now she wishes she'd had that piece of lemon pie."

Remember Aunt Lillian's joke: it's more than a joke.

Perhaps Uncle Drum's is too, but at this point I can't tell. I can only tell you what I heard because the next thing I knew there's this sweet man on the six o'clock news saying, "I tried to stop. I tried, but my foot couldn't find the brake." And sixty thousand husbands watching turned to sixty thousand wives and lovers and said, "I bet he did. I just bet he tried real hard." They'd been married for forty-six years.

Uncle Drum met Aunt Lillian at a USO dance during the war when he was stationed in Mississippi. She said she saw him across the room and thought he was the handsomest man she'd ever seen. "I still do," she said softly that Sunday afternoon before she was killed. We looked over an old photograph album found in the attic. "Tall and dark and handsome," she said. And he still is, with a little help from Grecian Formula 44. Her own hair varies from pink-red to red-lavender to orange-lavender. It would be cotton white if she didn't fool with Mother Nature.

You wonder about that day. The laws of Nature and fate.

How much of our lives is really an accident? How much can we actually control? Change? Prevent? Did Aunt Lillian, somewhere in her strange little psyche, really want to die? And Uncle Drum? Did he secretly sometimes wish she wasn't there? Didn't he, without knowing it, become an instrument in her suicide pact?

She was there all right. In the wrong place at the wrong time, or so the kinder people said, shaking their heads. It was an awful thing, a terrible thing to have happen. And the car? Everyone wonders about the car. Where is it now? Will Uncle Drum keep it? Will he sell it? What?

Then there's daughter Gloria. Who picked her up at the airport? What did she say and who told her? How would you tell someone her mother was dead? Her mother who had sailed through a mastectomy and back now lies cold on somebody's stainless steel slab of a table? Did Aunt Lillian know what happened? How conscious was she before the ambulance came and slid her in?

One of the neighbors, who saw the whole thing, heard Aunt Lillian scream and said she looked up as she lay there, shook her fist at him and said, "Drum, dammit, now you've done it. You've finally killed me."

Nobody said what Uncle Drum was doing during this time.

Did he try to hold her? Was she torn and bleeding? Did he stand there in shock and disbelief? Did he call her name and try to hold her back to keep her from dying? Was there a lot of pain or was she dead before the pain had time to hit?

The phone message I'd gotten said only that Aunt Lillian was dead and come as soon as I could, which I did, assuming all along the way a thousand things that could have happened. Heart attack. Stroke. Even suicide.

Aunt Lillian was not a stable person, not that I ever knew she'd attempted anything even resembling suicide. She was a family therapist, which she always said with a sharp crack of a little laugh. "That's a joke if I ever heard one." She had degrees from Duke, was trained and licensed. Had her own practice with a closed list of patients.

I know she was a sympathetic listener. She helped you field your way through days that were trapped with mines by asking the right questions, throwing a little spotlight underneath a rock you'd overturned, rousing up the rattlers. She was good at this, respected, read papers before national associations. Some of the most respected people in Durham were on her couch. Which she thought was a joke too.

"What they don't know," she used to say, "is blind leading blind."

Her own depression, a personal thundercloud she kept at bay, closer at times than others, then pushed away, had gotten worse lately. She wore no color but black, burned no light bulbs over 60 watts in any overhead or lamp in the house, kept blinds and curtains closed, and shrouded all the furniture in black-green throws she made herself. She was a case. "Boredom, boredom, boredom," I heard her scream once, "thy name is boredom."

We had eaten at the nicest restaurant in town. Uncle Edward in his Hickey Freeman suit had picked up the tab. There had been ten of us. Now dwindled to five finishing coffee. Uncle

Edward, Aunt Helen, his wife, Uncle Drum, Aunt Lillian, and me.

Aunt Lillian bypassed the lemon pie. She sat and shredded the red paper napkins she'd asked the waitress to bring, rolled them into balls, then tossed the balls at the wall. "Am I embarrassing you?" she asked Uncle Drum at one point.

"Not in the least," he said.

"I'll keep on, then," she said, turned away from the rest of us and kept rolling and tossing.

People in the restaurant stared and whispered.

Aunt Lillian shrugged, kept tossing.

Aunt Helen held her thick cloth napkin tight to her lap as though Aunt Lillian might run out of paper napkins and start on the real ones.

When we left, the floor looked as if it was splotched with blood.

Aunt Helen was disgusted and muttered as she went out the door, "A grown woman. A grown woman."

Uncle Edward gave the waitress an extra twenty dollars, indicated with a nod it was for whoever had to clean that table and was surely sorry to have been a party to such goings on.

Gloria, Uncle Drum and Aunt Lillian's daughter hadn't been around in years. Their only child, she'd gone off to college and never come back. Eventually she married a native of Washington state, had two children and still wrote only when she wanted money. Gloria never laughed. She never told jokes, but here's the joke. She loved comic books. Even as an adult.

The last time she was in Durham for a visit, she went shopping with me and what did she buy? Comic books. I couldn't believe it. Here she was wearing something that made a burlap bag look tailored and she bought comic books. And a supply of bubble gum. Enough to drive her mother crazy.

"Is this for the girls?" I asked Gloria.

"It's for me," she said. "They don't like it. I can't imagine. I've always lived on this stuff, but they won't touch it."

Whenever Aunt Lillian, Uncle Drum and Gloria came to visit when we were growing up, she traveled with the back seat full of comic books. Their car would pull into our driveway. Uncle Drum and Aunt Lillian would get out, hug my brother and me, and they'd go into the house. Richard and I would get in the car, sift through the comic books to see which ones we hadn't read ... which was probably most of them ... Gloria always had the latest ones ... go in the house, get ours to trade. Gloria flipped through them with a snort of disgust because they'd been read and were no longer fresh and shiny. Then the three of us sat in the car and read comic books for hours. Hours. Even in cold weather. We sat there in coats and sweaters for hours, not talking, the only sound in the car our breathing, an occasional sigh, cough or sneeze, and the turning of pages.

My parents were horrified. They said we were rude to Gloria and it wasn't healthy. We should either come in the house and play board games or get out of the car and run and play.

Those were always mother's words, "Run and play." To her the three words ran together.

Aunt Lillian always shrugged her shoulders, said "Let them do what makes them happy. At least they're quiet."

Uncle Drum only smiled. Gloria was clearly a foreign creature to him. He let Aunt Lillian raise her. His job had him on the road five days a week. Four weeks a month. He was only home for Christmas and Thanksgiving holidays. Weekends. I've often wondered if Gloria would have been different if Uncle Drum had been there more. And thought since, as an adult, how afraid Aunt Lillian must have been all those nights alone. How she said every appliance waited until Uncle Drum had driven out past the city limit sign on Monday morning to break down. How Gloria never had a fever on the weekend. How the worst storms and the hardest rain that pulled down tree limbs and lifted up roof shingles and found cracks to flood basements came during the week. How car batteries died on Monday mornings and a thousand other household disasters lay in wait for her alone.

I've remembered too, how she hated to drive. How she shook behind the steering wheel a few times I rode with her, how slowly she drove, waiting twice as long as she had to at stop signs and intersections, even on small trips to the grocery or drug store.

I've thought too, that she was the only person I knew who was really addicted to caffeine, truly addicted. Aunt Lillian always had a cup of coffee at hand. I have a picture in my mind too, of the times I've watched her dance and shake while she waited for a fresh pot of coffee to perk. She couldn't keep her feet or hands still.

After Uncle Drum retired, Aunt Lillian did too, retaining only one couple from her patient list. "They'd kill each other if they didn't have someone to go to every week and blow off steam. This way they can each save up all the slights and put downs and wham them at each other in front of me. I'm their audience and I charge them plenty, believe you me," Aunt Lillian said.

"How long have they been married?" I asked her once.

"Long enough to have all these things worked out long ago," she said and poured herself more coffee.

She and Uncle Drum worked out separate routines, together routines, even lunch and dinner menus that never varied. He puttered in his basement workshop. She painted in her basement studio. He cooked breakfast. She cleaned up. She made a tuna salad lunch. He cleaned up. They alternated weeks on dinner clean up.

Aunt Lillian painted in oils. The same subject. Magnolia blossoms. She said she was going to paint them until she got them right. I thought every one of her paintings looked alike. She framed and hung them all over the house. You ate looking at magnolias. You slept looking at magnolias. You bathed or peed looking at magnolias. Sometimes you thought the whole house even smelled of thick, decayed magnolia blooms and dried, jagged leaves.

One painting Aunt Lillian painted was a magnolia tree with their old car underneath. Uncle Drum must have been the first owner of a Nash Rambler and the last. This one was twenty years old and once, when I had stayed overnight with them, got me to the airport over iced roads and through snow banks that stopped lesser vehicles. She even painted Uncle Drum at the wheel of the car, and later I thought how prophetic. How damn prophetic.

He had three other cars, one in each garage, but the Rambler stayed parked in the turn space off the driveway. Remember that. It has something to do with what happened.

He kept the Rambler covered with a tarp which was probably worth more than the car. When he finally bought a new car, it was a Rambler Ambassador. A big gray thing. It was shiny as a hearse, and I was only with him once when he drove it. That time I scrunched into my seat, prayed we'd get out the driveway without him backing into another car and then to the shopping mall and back without him hitting someone.

You had to back out of Uncle Drum's driveway into traffic that came around a curve you couldn't see. Aunt Lillian's job was to stand at the end of the drive, watch for approaching traffic, signal Uncle Drum it was safe to back, stand by the side of the road, and after he got into the road and, "Ready to roll" (as he said), quick jump in the car, slam shut the door and head out.

In Uncle Drum's defense, when he built the house, though it was on a sharp curve, the street was dead end. It was dead end until recently. Then it became a cut through between thoroughfares and the traffic flew by faster than the speed limit.

And true, Uncle Drum redid his driveway to include an L where you could back, then head out into the street and thereby take some of the danger out of that driveway. But he kept the old car parked there, the old car with its expensive tarp, so he never could use the turnaround. Maybe he actually liked the excitement of Aunt Lillian on the watch for traffic and him whizzing the car back, whirling it around and jumping in the shotgun on a stage coach in the old west. Maybe they liked that. They were big TV movie buffs. Aunt Lillian said they'd seen everything on TV at least twice and some things ten times. She could lip sync most of the *M*A*S*H* shows and any Western that came on.

Maybe there was a tiny trace of some element of that but the bigger fault, the real story behind the story, is Uncle Drum's stroke and the new car.

Uncle Drum woke up one morning unable to talk and with his complete right side numb. Aunt Lillian immediately called the neighbors next door, who she said were "True saints on earth if there are any." The Knights came and Jim, who later had his own stroke while standing on the curb talking as Uncle Drum raked leaves, was able to help Uncle Drum down the stairs, into a car and to the hospital. Aunt Lillian went too and stayed the whole week Uncle Drum was in the hospital. By this time she wasn't driving at all. The Knights brought her changes of clothes from home, the mail and did all the errands that had to be done.

Within a few days Uncle Drum's speech was back. The first thing he said was "I want out of here." He regained use of his arm, then his leg, though he still walks with a limp. And he seems in general to go in a mode of slow motion. He seems to have to think through each move before he begins it.

Yet, he insisted on driving. You wonder if Aunt Lillian had still been driving things would have been different. But here his old macho male ego reared up and said, "I may not be able to do everything I want to, but by damn, I can still sit behind the wheel of a car, steer and stop it." Except he really couldn't.

Or maybe he could handle the old Nash. He said it was the new car's fault. He could have stopped the old car but his new one shot out from under him. No one will ever know.

What everyone who reads the area newspapers, maybe even the wire reports that went all over the country, or watches the eleven o'clock newscast, had heard about a man who backed out his own driveway over his wife of forty-six years and killed her.

This was two months after he'd had a light stroke. Time enough for them to get some papers in order, wills made and decide to do a little something for themselves in whatever time they had left. The stroke put a scare into them. "More like a royal fright," Aunt Lillian said.

Uncle Drum blamed the car. "I couldn't find the brakes," he said over and over and over. To the police who came out, the ambulance, the newspaper reporter and the television people who shoved a microphone under his nose. He just kept saying, "I couldn't find the brakes. My foot wouldn't move."

And all the husbands watching the eleven o'clock news or reading the newspaper said to themselves and out loud. "I just bet he couldn't. I just bet his foot wouldn't move." They probably gave wry laughs. Little cutting laughs and looked at their wives of ten years, or twenty-two years or thirty-seven years. Looked and wondered how much accident there really was in an accident.

Neighbors and friends of forty-six years came in and took a look. They helped Uncle Drum plan a memorial service. The called my cousin Gloria on the West Coast. They said her first reaction about her father. Had he had another stroke? When told it was her mother she'd said, "Thank God. I couldn't bear it if anything else happened to my daddy." Gloria had always been a daddy's girl, clinging to his arm, attaching herself to his side like a barnacle even after she was grown and had her own children. When she learned it was her mother who was found dead, there was just silence and she didn't ask when or how, just said tell her daddy to wire her money for a plane ticket and she'd catch the first one she could.

Neighbors met her at the airport, where they said she got off the plane looking like something left over from the Sixties. Khaki pants, jacket and tee shirt and carrying a back pack. No suitcase. No make-up case. No sign of a dress she might wear to her mother's funeral. And her hair looked like it hadn't seen a shampoo in a good number of weeks. But the worst offense was her shoes. She wore rubber-thonged flip-flops.

The neighbors thought surely somewhere in that backpack she had some decent shoes. Well, it turned out she didn't. Though they took her to the mall and helped her choose a baggy suit (it was the closest thing to a khaki color she could find and made her skin look sallow, slightly green tinted), she refused to try to buy shoes and ended up wearing those flip-flops to her mother's memorial service. Then later to the cemetery.

On the way to the cemetery she wouldn't ride in the car with her father (who she screamed at). "You killed my mother. How could you do such a thing? You killed her. You idiot." She beat on her chest when he tried to calm her down, to hug her.

Then, after the service at the gravesite, which was a couple of sentences from a minister Aunt Helen knew and would later remind Uncle Edward to tip two hundred dollars or so, the funeral director started to usher the family to the waiting cars when Gloria screamed out, "I'm not going until I see what I came for."

The funeral director leaned over and whispered to her and she said some things back and planted her flip-flop-shod feet firmly in the loose soil, refused to move.

Gloria watched the urn with her mother's ashes in the cherry wood box placed in the open earth and covered to a mound. Gloria watched every shovel full of dirt thrown on that box and in that hole and patted neatly and rounded smooth before she was satisfied. Then she got in the car, pulled out some comic books she'd bought at the mall and began to read. I'm willing to bet somewhere Aunt Lillian laughed.

As I said, in my family we don't tell stories, we tell jokes.

Snip Snip: Part I

The Woman Who Loved Her Hair

Every night for the past two weeks I've had the funniest feeling. Woke up with it. Like I'm not alone in my bedroom. That someone is in the room with me and yet I know there can't be. I have locks I always check and double check before I go to bed. When you live alone, you can't be too careful. Still, I have this feeling.

So far I haven't gotten up and turned on the light, but I could swear I hear breathing that isn't mine. I get wide-awake and watch the shadows. Nothing moves except the cat. She seems to tense up, raise her ears and listen, but then she's an old cat and I've known her to have nightmares, to wake up with a start, even run in place, digging all four feet in the air, twitch her whiskers like crazy. I knew dogs did that in dog dreams, and I've seen Clarisa do it during the day, so why not at night?

Or is somebody really there?

The shadows I've watched, tall, bulky and ill-figured on my closet door, turned out to be a wool robe, so soft and warm I wear it all year. It's like a baby blanket and after a hot bath, the dearest comfort (next to Clarisa) in the world. The other strange shadow, and I had to remind myself several nights straight, was not some looming, tall stranger, but merely my pink straw hat hung high on the Chinese Fortune jar atop my carved cherry highboy. I stuck that straw hat over the neck of the jar last summer for lack of any place else to throw it. And there it stayed.

When the curtains move from the force of air outside, I just take a deep breath and tell myself how healthy the freshness is. Deep breathe. Deep breathe.

When nothing moves, the cat relaxes, yawns (I feel the warm moisture from her mouth beneath my hand). I convince myself the only breathing in the room is me after all and I go back to sleep.

Still, there are times during the day even that I remember the feeling of being watched. Of not being alone.

When I brush my hair and pull it up with a twist, then pop in the combs to hold it, I feel eyes at my back. Almost a warmth of two penlights boring into my back. I swirl around and there's nothing, nobody there.

My hair is my best feature. Everyone says so. It's never been cut. Not in my whole life. Except once. I take that back. When I was twelve or thirteen, I got back this wild notion I wanted my hair short, that my headaches were caused by all that hair hanging so heavy from my scalp, so I went into a beauty shop and said whack this stuff off. Go to the roots if you have to, I told the beautician. She stood there in a pink-striped smock, scissors in one hand, and refused to do it without calling my mother first. Which I wouldn't do. Somehow Mama'd come flying from wherever she was and jerked me out of that shop and screamed at me for hours. Cried how I was committing sin and what all the Bible says. Daddy didn't bother to speak to me for days and days.

All my friends, however, liked it and I even got asked for the first and only date I've ever had in my life: Louis Felker, a redheaded boy with blue eyes and ten thousand freckles. I'd rather have hair than freckles any day. Lord, those things don't ever go away and hair you can do so much with. Long, you can. Short, I just gave up and waited for it to grow.

My hair's always been soft as silk, and I sleep with it loose, flowing around me like a cape. It warms me. And there's joy in brushing, which I do every night. Sometimes half an hour or more. This is what my mother did every night of my life until she died. I used to almost go to sleep when she brushed my hair, down and down my back. The feel of those tender bristles sang and soothed the most delicious end to a day.

Sometimes I felt the breeze at night lift my hair gently as any lover. Lift and let loose. Lift and let loose. It will put you right to sleep.

Once in a shopping mall, a woman with a clipboard tapped me on my shoulders from behind, said something about doing a survey on a shampoo and hair care products and if I could spare fifteen minutes of my time there was a nice prize in it for me. Then when I turned around she got a good look at my face, she stammered and said she was sorry but the survey said you had to be between the ages of 18 and 25. Of which I was neither. Except she didn't say that. From the looks of her, I could tell she thought it wasn't fair for hair like mine to be on somebody like me, and she was sorry the rest of me didn't go with it.

My favorite story growing up was Rapunzel: let down your hair. I could see my hair being twined into two ropes so that anyone could climb the ladder. If I wanted, except I can't imagine anyone I'd let in. I'm an extremely private person. I live alone, if you don't count Clarissa, and I like it, a lost lamb going through the world alone. A lost lamb going through this world alone and bald. It would be too awful to believe.

Snip Snip: Part II

His Mother Who Knows and Tells It Like It Is

It's not like heads. Look at it that way. And it doesn't hurt. Not that I'd want any of that hair on my walls, but then Burt's got his own place and I can't see myself telling him how to run it ... his business or his life. But I will tell you this, Flowburt had always been the oddest child. I know his name didn't help, didn't start things off right, but that was not any of my doings. His daddy, what he had of one, stayed around long enough to see he got here, weighed and named for a great uncle that fought and died during the last war, then he up and left for Alaska. You think I'd want to go live some place that's like the inside of a deep freeze? Not with my sensitive skin. Not with my asthma.

Oh, he sent money. Always been good about that. I never complained. Wasn't somebody I'd want to live with every day of my life anyway? And I had Burt. Burt was a good boy. An easy child to raise. He just had his ways and if you left him alone, no trouble, liked to be by himself, went to the library from the time he could read and walked there by himself, checked out books. Faye Cook'd called me from the front desk, say do you want me to let this boy check out this book and I'd say what book is it? And she'd rattle off some title about unsolved crimes or serial killers of the world or hidden treasures of the underworld and I'd say what harm can it be? He can't read it. But I guess he did. For a while he went around digging holes in any place anybody would let him, woods nobody owned, creek banks and fields. Found some arrowheads, some rocks that might be them. I never could tell, but that's what Burt would come home all excited about, wash and soak rocks in the basement sink. I let him do what he wanted as long as it didn't cost money. He never got into trouble, and I don't think he will now. It's just a little hobby. Not like most, but there's no harm in it. Not that I'd want all that mess hanging on my wall, but as I said, it's his wall and if he likes it and wants to live with it and nobody's getting hurt, then it's his business. Odd business, but his own. And Burt is a good boy. Why, most of my friends would give everything they got to have a boy as thoughtful and kind as mine. Never forgets my birthday. Took me to the Top of the Tower for dinner and we looked out and down below and had the finest time. The night was all black and diamonds and he gave me another pearl for my necklace. A real one. You can tell if you know how, but most people don't. If you drop a real pearl in a glass of water, it will stay at the bottom. If it's glass or plastic, it will rise to the top. I don't go dropping a real pearl in a glass of water, but it's nice to know I can if I want to and it will stay there.

Not a Mother's Day goes by that he hasn't sent me flowers so big the truck had to back up to the door to unload. I fuss at him just a little, spending all that money for something that doesn't last longer than a week, but he hugs me and says he's only got one mother. Words like that, things I like to hear.

And every week he does my hair.

I go down to his shop on Saturday nights, after everybody's left and he's finished for the day, and he'll shampoo and blow me dry and people at church the next day say I look like a picture. My hair naturally waves, if it's cut and styled right. Now it's white all over. I got something better than anything ever come from a bottle.

You know, I got his baby curls yet. Had a picture made from them. Maybe that's where he got the idea. There was a picture made from hair my grandmother had in her front room. Looked like a vase of flowers, but it was shades of hair. Work of art. Always caught people's attention. So when they had grandma's estate sale I made up my mind if anybody got that hair picture, it was going to be me.

My cousin Fanny Runyon (we used to call her Onion) thought she would have it and kept bidding opposite of me. I made up my mind to pay fifty dollars if I had to. It was like she knew that figure was in my mind all along. I knew she didn't have fifty dollars or even forty-nine, and we could have played cat and mouse all day but I was going to win. I got the picture. That's the one thing in the house Burt wants too. Of course, he'll get everything I've got and I've given him any furniture he's wanted, which hasn't been much ... just the den sofa, his bedroom suite and the mahogany secretary with the ball and claw feet. But the hair picture is a curiosity and I'm hanging on to that even if I do get tired of dusting it once a week in that dark hall. Looking at curls of hair made into shapes of flowers and ferns is interesting, thinking who all the hair come off of, who all wore them first, where they went, how they lived and died.

Once I took the frame off, glued down Burt's little baby curls that were blonder than anything on the dark old picture, but somehow fitted right in with all the reds and browns and blacks. You'd never know hair came in so many colors. I wanted to keep Burt's curls that were always so cute on the back of his neck. I cried the first cut he had. Cried and carried those curls home in my pocket. Of course, his hair never curled again and these are the only proof I've got it ever did. So I'm hanging on to that picture. You can't hang on to your babies after they grow up, but you can keep little things. I can't be blamed for that.

Snip Snip: Part III

I can't tell you how this kicks up my life. The thrill of the find, some of them are so ordinary in every other way, then planning out the way I'll do it. At times it seems every fiber in my body gears up. I tingle so I can hardly sleep. I feel electric and glowing all over. Like a light bulb. I wonder everybody can't see it. See me radiating excitement as I get things more and more into place and practice, I practice several times in the weeks before I do it. Practice getting into the house, whether it's by a clumsy lock on a door or a window that won't quite shut or one that stays open. You'd be surprised at the people who have to sleep with a window open, even in the coldest weather. All it takes for me is a crack. Just enough to get my fingers under and ease the glass up, then slide myself in. I work out every day so I stay slim as a snake and agile. I oil my way in and once in, I can move quieter than air. I practice that at home, using taping equipment that will pick up anything. Even breath. I learned to breathe behind the black stocking, to see through the smallest slits for light. And to be quick. My moments are magic. Some of them never know until morning and then they don't believe their mirror, what they don't hold in their hands. Seeing isn't believing to them. Sometimes that's when they come crying into my shop and there is nothing I can do at that point, but shape them up a little. A snip here, then tell them they never looked better in their lives. For some that's the truth, but they act like hair was all they had. Their today, mine tomorrow I could say, but of course I don't. I let them cry on my shoulder, get my plastic capes all sticky with tears and stories. Who could ever have done such a thing? How unthinkable such an act is. How horrible. Who would want hair? Who would sneak into someone's bedroom late at night when they are asleep and cut off their hair? Who? Who? Who? They cry.

And I can't answer, of course. What's hair? Why, it's something living and breathing and growing back at the very moment they are crying and carrying on up a storm. Of course it will take years to reach the lengths they have lost, maybe never. Not for the older ones, but what was it to them anyways? The hair was too good for them. It didn't belong on them. It belonged to something, for something lasting, something permanent. I plan a hair museum of the finest *real* tresses in the world. And I've gone all over getting them. In some countries, you can see a woman on the street with hair.

That is not your everyday thing. Meanwhile, my life is full of excitement and danger. One without the other would be enough for most, but not me. Two is delicious for words, so don't listen for me or my scissors.

You won't hear either. Until you wake.

The Artist's Story

I painted the sign pink, but I wrote the message in purple: "Go to Hell, Gloria Deshaun." I debated whether to include the comma, but figured Miss Miseemer would surely walk by and if she did, she'd ring my doorbell, poke her finger in front of my face and let me have it full force. Tenth-grade English. She taught the whole town and never lets you forget it. So I put in the comma in honor of Miss Miseemer. Then I planted the sign, which was tastefully done, I might say, prominent in my wildflower bed, tilted at the perfect angle for glorious Gloria to see every time she so much as aims her head out her prissy Dutch door. Which always reminds me of a horse stall. And you can't convince me it's authentic anyway. Nobody but Gloria Deshaun would stand half in and half out of a conversation, all the while pretending to be half in and half out of everything that's going on. Having a place to duck if the poo poo happens to fly. Which is why her phone call surprised me.

There I was last Friday morning, out on my early morning deck, birds going full blast soprano around me, flowers blooming their perfect little buds off, bees doing bee things, a whole pot of magnificent coffee, a fresh newspaper and me at total peace with the world. I thought, Frederick James Allen Claymore Poole (Mama knew I'd be the only one, and absolutely only son, so she used all the family names at once), this is on the road to as good as it gets and you are one lucky, living, breathing SOB. Life is delicious.

Then the phone rang.

And this sweet voice dripping with the scent of magnolias and wet as April dew came out and licked my ear. "All of us on Eleanora Earlham Pinckney Street want you to know we appreciate whatall you've done to your house and how everything you've done to enhance your property has so greatly enhanced *ours*." She emphasized "ours."

I listened.

She paused. *She*, being the Gloria Deshaun of *the* Howard Deshauns of *the* historical committee and any other committee she could get her ass on. I, being sometimes more a fool than others, even had the flickering thought that me and my house were actually being invited to be on the annual tour, which has turned out to be the twice annual tour so *the* historical bitches can play tea party two times a year and count in double the money. But it's a good cause. Even if I do know those whose homes are chosen for the touring have to work their butts off and get nothing for it but dirty carpets, handprints on brass (which has to be polished, polished), and crushed grass if you include your garden. I'd have doubts about doing mine; people have been known to pick things when no one is looking and you can't be looking *every* minute. But while I was considering, even a teeny, tiny bit of considering, the white Karo voice went on.

"... and that's why I hesitate to say anything."

"What?" I put my coffee pot back on the warmer and turned up my attention. Opened it wide up. I was flat out listening now.

"Your front yard is not in keeping with the city ordinance."

"Who says?" I said, figuring she's got some eensy niggling thing on her inch-deep mind. Make that half-inch. What could she know about city ordinances? This fifty-year-old debutante still dreaming her debutante dreams? You know the ones. They never recover.

"Why, Claymore, the city ordinance that specifically specifies yards that have weeds or other noxious vegetation 24 inches high violate the city code."

"I have no weeds," I said. Surely this woman was not talking about me and certainly not my yard. I keep my grass clipped. There's so little of it, I could do it on my knees with Mama's sewing scissors. Dry, of course. I wouldn't want to take a chance on rust.

"You have fifteen days to trim it back or appeal."

"Trim what back, Sugar?" I said. I take my coffee black and strong and poured myself some now. In my mind I tried to review what on earth this woman with a lollipop in her mouth could possibly mean. The limbs on my trees are graceful and hanging low, but they're old and there's so few, I don't want to go doing nasty things to them. My grass looks like it was rolled out and patted into place and my borders are doing what borders do. They're thick and lush and full of color. The place is a show with hummingbirds in and through like little green arrows, butterflies lifting and flickering like flowers borne on the breeze. There's not a thing I want to change or trim. I love my gardens front and back.

"You can trim it or appeal." Gloria's voice suddenly had scratches in it. Static. Like a distant storm brewing.

"There's not a thing growing in my yard they don't have down at Lanier Park by the dozens, by the hundreds and thousands and I don't hear anybody telling them they got to trim. Trim! The very word cuts my mouth."

"Your yard is a sight," Gloria said. The way she said the word was sharp and crisp. Slick as a knife blade. The nerve of that woman attacking my yard. Her words, that voice. They hit me like a hammer. My shoulders began to shake.

"Foxgloves," I said. "Darling love, little dear, you don't trim foxgloves. They'd be ruined." And I thought, how futile, how futile to try to educate someone who insists on remaining dumber than a rock. Oh Lord. I was not going to trim my precious foxgloves for anything. There had been two years getting them to bloom and they were waist high. Why, what would the hummingbirds do? What would they do?

I didn't like laying on the darlings, the sweetenings, but sometimes that melts the frost off some of these old refrigerators.

"It's all of it," Gloria went on. "You can hardly see your house for that mess."

"Mess? Mess? People see my house all winter long." I felt myself getting close to a scream, so I spoke slower, more calmly. "In summer, I want to give them color and light. I want to be the Monet of Merony. I suppose even the ivy bothers you too." I knew perfectly well she had more ivy in her yard, leaf for leaf, than I'd ever have. What I hoped hers had, and mine didn't, was a cool little ropey nest of slinky striped garter snakes waiting to climb zip, zip up her skirt.

"No," Gloria said, "ivy isn't the issue here and you know it. What do you take me for?"

"I take you for somebody who's got her nose where it don't need to go." Sometimes I use the common English for emphasis. I've discovered some people in the shop find it perfectly charming. Yankees. They give each other a little sideways smile as if to say we got us a real little bubba here. One just touched a bit with a brush of talent.

"Fifteen days," she said and hung up the phone.

Click. Just like that. Little Miss Margarine Mouth. Little Miss Lizard Breath. I put down my coffee, rolled up that newspaper and looked for something to swat. Oh, if there was something close by I could just hit hard as hell. I knew I'd feel a little better.

Then I thought of a thousand things I wished I'd said. Isn't it always that way? Why, last week *Better Yards and Gardens* had been all over this place, every inch outdoors with their cameras and screens and lights. You wouldn't think outdoor shooting would need lights, but they do. And there I was with the spray bottle freshing up any plant that showed a single sign of even thinking of wilting. It took all I could do to restrain myself when they put glue on my roses. Dripped clear glue so it looked like dew and even if it did ruin those roses, my picture perfect "Perfections," I knew they'd be worth it in the magazine.

But, blast, did that historical committee think I was going to sit back and let them ruin my yard? Cut down my living, my life in the prime? Not a minute.

I emptied my coffee grounds among the roses, petted every foxglove on its head, and went to the back porch for gardening shears and my new basket. I'd used Mama's old flat basket for gathering all these years, then two months back, some ladies saw it, twittered over it, had to have it or die, I let it go. Felt like I was selling Mama, I'd seen her hands on that handle so often. But I parted with it. Mama would have laughed and laughed at what I got for it. She taught me to put a price on things and never be surprised at what people were willing to pay if they saw something they liked.

This is my living that historical committee is messing with, I said and snipped carefully a Queen Anne's lace here, a black-eyed Susan there, a coreopsis, a rudika, a start flower, some bronze fennel, sprays of fleabane. I could have lost myself in that meadow of my yard and been so full of sunshine and flower honey I'd float straight up. But I didn't.

Three hours later, after I'd finished my watercolor of "May Morning," those flowers in a basket, I put both in the shop, the painting on a small easel and the flower arrangement in the window. The painting would be sold by three and the basket too. Sometimes the same person buys both. "One to enjoy now," they say and hold the basket up, "and the other forever."

Glorious Gloria has no idea what it takes to keep up a house these days. She has a round little husband bringing home the cheese and bread. And I have only me. This house and my garden. Thank God, Mama had sense enough to buy a corner lot and I could get it all zoned for business. More Paintings and Things is something Mama must have seen in her crystal ball, because after I came back from Pratt, where I found they couldn't teach me a thing, but I did so enjoy the museums, clubs and things, I set up a studio in the old front bedroom. Then after Mama passed, I let her bedroom, the sitting room, dining room and pantry all go into the makings of an antique business.

Of course my paintings, and all summer, May until October, my garden gives me additional income. Wildflowers are the rage these days. I've sold armloads to florists for weddings. Even a funeral spray. (I don't know what that said about the deceased and I don't want to know.) I can gather and pick and you can't tell they've been touched. They grow overnight, thick and into each other, masses of color. It's multicultural, I tell people. This is the way we should all be—one great, beautiful, blooming garden of humanity.

So where does Gloria the great, goodness gracious to all, Queen of the avenue, fit in? She's a pimple on the back ass of mankind. She's a gnat's navel. She's not worth the cuticle off my pinkie swear.

But she was gutsy. Made the first call. After that the others didn't do anything but make me madder. They disturbed my sleep, my mornings on my back deck, my daily life. And the wildflowers knew it. They seemed subdued. I had less blooms, more seed heads. They got leggy, looked tired.

I took the phone off the hook, hid it under one of Mama's second-best quilts. Put the portable down there with it. For company.

Then I went to see my lawyer, Ritchie Lee Otis.

R.L. said, "Claymore, you can't fight city hall."

I cried on his desk until it and I were all soppy wet, and all he did was ask his secretary for paper towels and a glass of water. When she brought it, the towels didn't look all that clean, so I pushed myself up off that desk and left, totally damp and disgusted.

That night I dreamed I saw Mama in the garden. The flowers almost hid her, but I'd know that beautiful face anywhere, that angel voice. "Baby," she said, "cut the flowers, gather them up in bunches and hang them up to dry. You can sell them all winter long and double your money.

Put the price up there. Put them in baskets, hang them in handfuls on the walls tied at the waist with a toss of ribbon and you'll sell, sell, sell. Let them think they won. The flowers will come back and be thicker than ever. Wildflowers thrive on adversity. They're like us, darling boy." She blew me a kiss and was gone.

The fourteenth day I waited until high noon in broad daylight, then cranked up the mower I rented, a big, green tractor of a thing and pretended I was Farmer Brown cutting hay on the north 40. Oh, the smell of the green souls of all those plants as I went round after round. Their life juices clung to me like an opaque veil, thick and sticky. But I couldn't shower just yet. Not until I finished the job.

I did one more thing I hope Mama sees. Wherever she is. I did it for her.

That night, at the silver hour, that time just before dawn when the dark is giving way and day starts to climb that big hill behind the Catholic Church, I hauled a dozen bags of rock salt one by one down to Glorious Gloria's wide, rolling expanse of lawn.

When I bought the rock salt in Elm City, the man said, "Somebody fixing to have a big ice cream social?"

And I said, "The biggest."

I walked up and down on little Gloria's gracious, spacious lawn that was mowed smooth as carpet and soft as such. I spelled out a great big B with curls and swirls, then followed it with an "itch."

Not a soul stirred in the neighborhood. Not a dog barked as I coasted down the street to my bare lawn that looked scalped. Raw and lonely and still bleeding green. Tomorrow I'd gather armloads of the sweet things, arrange them in families and groups of friends, then hang them in the attic to dry. Oh, a great big attic is a wonderful thing.

And comes a good rain, all those seeds I mowed will get going zoom, zoom on a second growth and Gloria will see how you spell her name another way.

The Hairdresser's Story

All I had was the name Blue and Shoeman Farm Circle off Thunder Mountain Road. And though I've lived in this county all my life, I'd never heard of either. So I called Everhart at the county office. He's mapped every pig path and dogtrot in every corner of this county.

"Everhart, hon," I said. "Mabel here, you ever heard of Shoeman Farm off Thunder Mountain Road?"

"Thunder Mountain." He laughed a great big laugh. "That place is so wild they keep polecats for housepets."

"I meant Shoeman Farm Road," I said.

Right off, real quick, he said, "Not in this county. Not to my knowledge. But if you find it, be sure and let me know."

I said I would and checked my map again. Nothing. Not even a dogleg of a line that led off Thunder Mountain Road that wound all along the river. I decided to chance it. To get out of that shop and those four walls on a yellow October day sounded like a picnic to me.

I go where they call me. Rich houses, poor. Treat them all the same. Charge them alike. Mostly. They all leave feeling twice what they were when they crawled in my door. They say, "Mabel, your four fingers have a magic touch." And truth to tell, sometimes I do feel a tingle or two in the tips.

I'm one of the few left in this world who make house calls of any kind. Somebody lets you into their house, they let you into their lives. At least a room or two.

Sometimes that's as far as I want to go. Red and black plush bedrooms of old ladies. Pink fancy frilly boudoirs of single men. You'd be surprised what I see and have seen.

Elderly people who have floral drapes, recliners big as pickup trucks and brown linoleum floors covered with throw rugs stained with poodle pee. I've been in them all. But I truly don't do miracles, and if things keep going the way they are, I'll have to change the name of my shop to "Better Beauty" or "Beauty Business" or something like that. This miracle business has nearly worn me out. Two weirdies in one day is two too many.

But I needed to get out of earshot of the details of Lucynelle's mama's dying. If she didn't get it over and done with soon, I was going to go out there and see if I couldn't help the woman along a little bit. To give Lucynelle credit though, not once has she asked me to put in for a miracle on her mama's behalf. She knows we don't do miracles. Not that I know of.

So there I was with my bag and curlers, in my new purple van, wheeling out the parking lot, not knowing where I was going any more than the cow jumping over the moon.

Life isn't always on the map, I told myself, leastways not mine. I knew if I heard about Lucynelle's mama's medications and constipations one more time, I was going to say something that would probably hurt her feelings and I'd have to do something great, big and fancy to get her back speaking to me. If I didn't find the road, I could always say I tried.

I drove down Main Street, where there was a mongrel dog in front of the bank licking himself like crazy. Lord, if John Sykes was alive, he'd be out there with a stick running it off.

I turned at Ray Poplin's Esso station, and next thing I knew I was out in open country. This county is still that way in a lot of places and I like it. I like pastures and barns and silos. Big white farmhouses where real people live. Give me those any day instead of fancy con-DO-min-e-yums. Big name for an apartment, I've always thought. Crowd people in too close and they get on each other's nerves. You don't have neighbors. You have a name and a number and know nothing about each other. I couldn't stand to live that way. Even if it did mean I wouldn't have to hear and know about Lucynell's mama's dying every day of my life.

When I went past William Watson's barbershop, I gave a great big toot with my horn and waved. William was sitting in his barber chair like he does most days. White shirt and tie. Sits and looks out the window. Watches traffic. Says, "Wish I had a dollar for every car that goes by" to anybody who's fool enough to stop in. William cuts hair the way they learned when he was in barber school thirty years ago and his customers have died off. Those that liked haircuts skinned to the scalp. And the line around their ears and across the back of their neck all white and naked looking. All the young people today go where they style and set or come to my shop for a trim or a perm. Never in my life thought I'd see the day I'd be giving perms to men and boys, but if that's what they want and they pay for it, they get it. Hair's hair, I always say. And I wouldn't be surprised if Jesus Christ himself were alive today, if he wouldn't stop by my shop for a trim and a blow dry.

William doesn't see it that way. The last time he came to my shop and accused me of stealing his customers I told him there was no stealing about it. I didn't go out on the street and drag them in. I didn't advertise I do men and boys. Word gets around, and if he wanted his business back he'd better get with it. Update his shop and change his way of cutting hair. He called me a conniving old hussy. He hissed the word between his two front teeth that are as big as a horse's. Then he curled his lip in a sneer and left, saying I hadn't seen the last of him.

Lucynelle started crying, said, "Mabel, you done it now. You got an enemy for life."

There wasn't a thing I could do about it. I hadn't done anything to start with and couldn't do anything to stop it. You don't turn away business, not if you know what's good for you.

At Wynonna's Florist, which is out by itself in an old service station building, I noticed she'd already put up her Christmas decorations. Tree and stuff. She leaves those little white twinkly lights on her bushes all year. I thought at first that was tacky, then decided it was a pretty good idea. Light up your place of business at night and it might keep it from getting broken into. Of course I take all cash home with me at the end of the day and Wynnona does too. But people today will break into any place where they think they might get something they could sell or trade. We don't live in the best of times, I say sometimes. But things could always be a lot worse. If you got your health, a little health insurance and work to keep your mind off things, then you got everything. Everything that counts.

When I passed by Eileen Tully's pasture I almost hit my brakes. She must have had a hundred sheep, all with little black masked faces, and there were lambs! Four or five of those. Cutest things in this world frisking around behind that white fence.

I don't get a chance to drive out in the country much and when I do sometimes I just want to keep going and going and going. Driving to the end of the earth. Which is where I felt like I was going.

Thunder Mountain was at the backside of the county anyway, and when I turned, the road was blacktop for a couple of miles. There I was looking right and left for a sign that said Shoeman Farm Road when I hit gravel. And dust. And the Graham County line. No wonder Everhart didn't know it. Wasn't our county. So I slowed, even if I was going slow to begin with and could have gotten stopped for looking like a drunk driver if there had been any cops within a hundred miles which there probably wasn't. I hung on to the steering wheel and thought how I was going to add a wash job onto the price of whatever it was I was going out there to do.

When Lucynelle took down the name and address, she could have written permanent or cut or wash and set on the Postanote. She didn't even write the time of the appointment. What if I drove all this way and nobody was home?

When I was almost in the mood to turn back, I saw a little hand-lettered sign behind the road. Blue. I wheeled in between two pretty looking ponds and followed a white fence with red cedars poking up like tent poles every ten feet. Next thing I knew I was climbing so steep I had to put the van in second. Still no house in sight.

I rounded a couple more sharp turns, and next thing I knew there was Tara. Or a house that looked like Tara in *Gone with the Wind*. Those tall white columns, that wide porch. A real mansion on a hill. So big it almost took my breath away. Heard myself swoon out loud. Lord dee!

When I cut off the motor, there wasn't a sound but the ticking as the engine cooled. Not a dog nor person came to meet me.

So I grabbed my bag, hoisted myself down and took a flagstone walk between boxwoods big as buildings. I've always loved the smell of boxwoods, so I took my time and took in the sights. A garden where a fountain splashed. A big fountain with a statue of a stone boy peeing to beat the band. There were lily pads and frogs and all. Even some late chrysanthemums blooming and fresh pansies freshly planted in beds here and there.

Not a soul in sight, so I meandered up to the steps, across the porch and started to ring the bell when the big door swung wide open and a little black girl with a thousand braids sprouting from her head stood there.

"Honey," I said, "you like to have scared the britches off me."

She had an orange and white cat big as a raccoon draped around her shoulders. "Papa Pete," she yelled behind her. "Somebody's here." Then she shut the door and there I stood until it opened again and a black man in a gray suit held out his hand. "Queen Esther will be so glad to see you."

He motioned me into a living room big enough for the spring cotillion. Three chandeliers dripping glass big as that fountain dripped water.

I followed him down a hall to a yellow bedroom where a woman lay propped in the biggest four-poster bed I've ever seen, a hundred pillows at her back. She turned away when she saw me.

"No use," Papa Pete said. "Here's your medicine for today. This'll make you well till tomorrow. Then tomorrow we'll have another tea party or two."

"Mabel Huggings," I said and went toward her, but she kept her head turned. I told him what I'd need, took off my coat and unpacked my bag, wondering what miracle I could wring out of these hands on that stubborn old head.

"Nothing to make you feel better like a clean head of hair." I put on my smock and rolled up the sleeves. "Best tonic money can buy."

I pulled out the pins and laid them on the night table at the foot of a lamp decorated with roses. It even had a pink bulb, so the whole room had a soft pink feel.

"When you look good," I said and started brushing her hair that now unrolled and crawled over the side of the bed like a gray striped snake, "you feel good. And we're going to get you feeling good."

When the man came back with the water, I lathered her up and began to work. The hair filled the basin and I asked for a bigger one.

He came back with a tin tub and that worked. Me soaping and rinsing, soaping and rinsing. Him holding her hand and singing her a little song under his breath.

I kept adding up what I was going to charge like a cash register in my head. This was one head of hair. When it was washed and I'd used a dozen towels to dry it as best I could, I got my blower going. Even then I knew I needed one stronger, so he let go her hand and brought in a little silver gun that didn't put out enough heat to warm an eyebrow.

I pulled a chair up to that bed, fanned her hair over the back of it and worked from the scalp down. Miss Queen just lay there with her eyes closed.

Even though her nightgown was buttoned at her throat with a little dot of a pearl, I could see there wasn't much to her. Skin and bones and a houseful of hair is all I could think.

Once she sighed and I said, "Honey, I know you're worn out, but I'm almost through and you're going to feel so much better. That hair was so full of its own oil, it weighted you down."

Her skin was thin as yellow paper and full of little blue lines like roads on a map. She wasn't long. Don't die under my hands, I kept thinking. Wait until I'm gone to do what you have to do.

Her breathing was like a purr, and my drier whined and whined as I moved it down and back, down and back, drying that head of hair. I could spread it out and it would have covered the bed.

"You ever think about having some of this cut off?" I asked the man who held both her hands in his.

He stiffened. "Queen Esther's glory is not for man to defile."

I could have bitten my tongue. People are so personal about hair. Picky. Quirky. Persnickety. It's just stuff. Living cells that will grow back. You can cut it, bleach it, dye it, twist it, roll it, do all kinds of things. Hair takes it. Perks up. Does stuff. Comes back if you treat it right. So I just kept drying and adding. A hundred dollars. This is worth at least a hundred dollars. Two. These people had it somewhere. You didn't live in a house like this with all this fine furniture and not have some money somewhere.

Finally I started two braids going. One on each side of the bed. Then I had her bend over as close to her knees as she could and I wound those ropes up as high as they'd go, pinning and pinning.

Then when she lay back against the pillows, she smiled. There was color to her cheeks, and for the first time I saw her eyes were round and blue as a robin's egg.

"You rest now," I said. "We've worn you out."

Truth to tell. I was worn out myself. And wet. My smock was wet through to my bra and panties. And I didn't have a stitch to change into. I'd run the heater on high all the way home and hope I didn't catch the "B-monie," as Lucynelle's little sister Gloria used to call it.

I hustled into my coat, packed up my gear and tiptoed out. Why I tiptoed on that thick white carpet, I don't know, but I did. And went looking for the old man and the child.

I followed the murmur of voices down a hall, through some dark paneled rooms with high windows and thick draperies, to a kitchen, where the child sat on her knees on a tall stool and the old man cut biscuits with the rim of a glass.

"Send your bill to Mr. William Watson," he said. "This is his playhouse." He laughed. "I'm his daddy and that's his mama back there in bed. This here," he patted the little girl on the head, "is something the cat brung up."

The little girl giggled.

William Watson. Mr. William Watson. All this going on and nobody knew a word. I hightailed it out of there and revved up my van loud enough to tell them in that kitchen I was not happy. Why couldn't William himself have come over to my shop and explained the situation? Then it would have been a different story. But here it was a trick. He got me and I'd never get paid for any of this unless I went storming into his shop and raised a whole bunch of hell, which I could do.

I roared past the barn, not thinking a thing except how mad I was and what all I was going to say to Mr. William Watson when I saw him. Then I saw him. Saw Elvis. On a motorcycle. Or somebody close enough to be his twin brother.

Then he was behind me on the black thing. Sunglasses. Leather jacket. All. It was Elvis if I had to stake my life on it. In my mirror that's what I saw until he passed right by me flying like the wind.

I shook all over. And it wasn't because I was cold. Two weirdies in one day was too much for any woman. I knew I hadn't done any miracles in his direction that day. Nor any other. Lord dee. Lord dee.

The Niece's Story

Dray thought the kitchen smelled like apples. Or roses? He couldn't decide. And some sort of spice. Cinnamon? He didn't know, only that the smells made him hurt, a pain that started in his chest, then steadied to a dull motor in his stomach.

"Take a chair," she said, after he handed her the pants. "I'll make us a pot of coffee."

"No," he said, "that's all right." He wasn't drinking coffee these days, just tea weak as dishwater. Instant and too sweet, but he liked the little bit of lemon taste as it was. She put the coffee on anyway and laid the four folded pairs of his pants on her sewing machine. He saw she'd moved a dozen African violets and a fern to open it. He hadn't meant to be so much trouble when he called to ask if she still sewed.

"A little," she said. "Nothing like I used to."

Nothing was like it used to be. He lived in a house so empty of noise the rooms talked to him and worse, he talked back, not saying words, but in his head. Walls that felt too small when the kids and Renita were there. They left one at a time, and the holes they made in his life were big as trees.

"Why, I used to sit down after supper, think nothing of it, and run up Bitsy Anne a new outfit before bedtime. I couldn't count the times I've done that. She'd get up the next morning and a new blouse and skirt would be hanging on her closet door like elves had left it." Helen laughed.

Renita had been like that. He'd gone to sleep more times than not to the buzz and rebuzz of Ree at her sewing machine, bent over some dress or shirt, or mending. She mended like nobody's business and toward the last quilted like a spider, threads weaving over each other until those squares hung together when you held them up, made patterns. There was a stack of her quilts in the closet he couldn't touch yet, and it had been seven months.

Helen cut two slices of a dark cake with white icing that stood in peaks and waves. She put a placemat in front of him: a scalloped placemat, blue plastic. The napkin matched, but it was paper.

He flipped the rounded corners with his fingers. "I ate."

"I know." Helen put a glass cover back over the cake. "But this is fresh and it dries out."

The cake was soft, light on his tongue, the icing like cream. He let it melt, run down the back of his throat in a thin, sweet stream. Lord, it was good. He ate almost all of it before touching his coffee. He'd eaten so fast he was ashamed. Now, only crumbs lay on his plate. He used his napkin.

"I didn't come for this," he said. The hot coffee steamed his glasses and made her face a framed blur.

"I know," she said, "but I've got it."

She cut him another piece, laid it on his plate gentle as feathers. He couldn't remember the last cake he'd tried. Bought cakes tasted like the inside of a box; frozen ones were just sweetened air and foam. He'd quit on sweets at all. He'd just about plain quit on food itself. None of it tasted right, no matter how much he salted and ketchupped it. Things were either raw or hard black like the stuff on the bottom of the oven. And tasted like it.

When he finished the second slice of cake, she said, "Let me get my tape measure," and slipped out of the room.

He scraped his fork over the plate, finished his coffee. Real coffee. It really made a difference. He felt satisfied. Even his stomach felt warm.

When she came back, he stood and she pulled the tape measure around his waist. He held up his pants with one hand while she measured.

"Couple more pieces of that cake and I wouldn't have to do this," she said.

No woman but his wife had touched him in so long. He stiffened at her fingers holding the inches.

"You lost forty pounds, I bet." She wrote down his measurements, pulled in her mouth. "Just the opposite of me."

She took her chair at the sewing machine. "When Farris died. I gained twenty." She unfolded his navy pants, measured and pinned. "I'll try to take them up so they won't bag on you."

"They're so baggy now, I'm ashamed to be seen. At least at church, I got a coat on to cover them ... all bunched up in the back." He played with his cup handle. Her kitchen was so light and clean. It shined.

He rubbed the wax on her tabletop. Plants in her windows bloomed and nodded among green stems and leaves. Ree's plants died. He didn't notice them until one morning they were all brown and falling into the sink. Even then, he hadn't thrown them out, just moved them over on the windowsill.

Outside Helen's window a bird red as a paper heart bounced on a limb full of fat buds. The bird sat warm in the sunshine and so did Dray, who'd never noticed the cold before this winter. Sleeping by himself, sometimes after he got into bed, he thought he'd never get warm.

Helen bent over the sewing machine, light on her work hands, white as doves, easing the material under and through the stitching. Dray watched the clock tick. In the other room, one chimed, and he thought the bells sounded golden, musical as an instrument played in church.

She held the pants up. "I took in as much as I could on that back seam. Try them on before I do the others. See how they fit." She handed the pants to him, indicated the bedroom and started pinning the next pair.

Her bedroom somehow made him feel like tiptoeing, the carpet thick and white. Her bed even felt fluffy when he sat on the side of it to take off his pants, pull on the altered ones. When he stood and looked in the mirror, he didn't see himself, just a thin man whose hair had more gray than him. He slicked it back, patted his waist, where the pants felt snug and fine. Just right. He walked back to the kitchen in his sock feet.

"How do they feel?" she asked, turning from the machine, her profile silhouetted by the light.

"Like new," he said. "Good for another thousand miles."

She smiled, started stitching the brown pants. He looked past her clean curtains and blinds out the window to the bird feeder. That red bird was still there, only now a yellow-brownish one pecked on the ground. He'd heard some birds mated for life. He didn't know why. All birds looked alike to him.

He started to pull off the pants she'd just fixed, then decided he'd wear them home. Let her work on the ones he wore here. Every pair he had was falling off. As long as he could remember, Renita had sewn what had to be stitched or fixed. She'd made his shirts too. First time he'd had to go buy one he couldn't tell the clerk what size. Funny, you just get to depend on things and don't pay attention when you need to.

When he straightened up from putting on his shoes, he studied the pictures on her dresser: Helen in her wedding dress, then Farris and their girls, then one each of the girls in graduation gowns and wedding gowns. The dark-haired one looked so much like Helen's wedding picture, he went back and studied it all over again. The younger one looked more like Farris. Then there were some little pictures of babies with birthday cakes and party hats. He picked up a photo, noticed it didn't leave a dust print. He never dusted until it got so thick he could roll it like fuzz from a blanket. He didn't notice until then.

Helen had finished the brown pants, folded, and stacked them on the table, started the tan ones. He stood in the doorway, holding the pants he'd worn here.

"Reckon you can take these up too ... while you're in the business?"

"Won't take me but a minute," she said, clipped her threads and held the tan pants out to him. "Trade." She laughed. "Even Steven."

Dray thought how much her laugh sounded like Ree's, the same little bells, and it hurt him remembering. Hurt like a splinter in his heart. And they looked alike, especially Helen at the sewing machine. Even from the back she reminded him of Ree. He put his dirty coffee cup and cake plate quietly in the sink, noticed that even her sink smelled clean like soap and lemon and sunshine. His own had black, deep odors that seemed to mold and escape into every corner of the kitchen. He'd like to ask her what she used, but didn't know how. He'd used so much stuff talked about on commercials, and nothing had done anything like the TV said.

When she handed him the stack of pants, the last pair altered and folded on top, he said, "How much I owe you?"

"Not one thing," she said.

"I got to pay you something." He patted his back pocket for his wallet. "Didn't come here for you to do all this for nothing."

“I’m glad to do it,” she said. “Glad to know I can still stitch up a seam or two. Maybe they’ll hold you for a while.”

“They’ll do fine,” he said, “but I don’t aim to go without paying you something.”

“I won’t take it.” She held her hand toward him like a policeman. “I mean it. As much as Ree did for me while she was alive. I wouldn’t think of it.”

He put the money, his wallet back, started out. "I thank you.”

“You’re more than welcome. Anytime.” She held the door for him.

When he started the car and backed out, he looked in his rearview mirror. Helen stood on the little porch, hands in her skirt pocket. He tooted the horn, waved, felt himself smile. She’d only fixed his winter pants. If he didn’t start gaining soon, he had about that many summer pants to need taking up. At the corner, he glanced back a last time. She was still on the porch, and he thought for all the world it was Ree all over again.

There were bugs in his oatmeal. Drayton put his hand in the box and watched black specks inch up his fingers. He poured the oatmeal out for birds, then checked the box of grits and poured it out too. He found bugs in the cornmeal, flour, cans of spices, even red pepper had bugs. He tossed out the lot, boxes of spaghetti, macaroni, noodles, everything opened and unopened, went into the trash. He pulled off yellow and brittle newspapers lining the shelves, January 12, 1951. He studied the car ads, read the sports section, didn't know a single name.

Dray stood looking at the bare shelves, then started on the refrigerator, throwing out bits of jelly left in jars, mustard, rusty-looking jars of mayonnaise, pickles. There were hard, black, lumpy glumps of things in the crisper. One might have been a cabbage once.

In the freezer he had ice trays, half a box of fish sticks and a can of pink lemonade. He threw that out. After he rolled the trash container to the street, he thought he felt weak and realized he hadn't eaten. He was hungry, so he got in the car and drove to Biscuit Town, ordered an egg biscuit to go. Then, changed his mind and went in. The only customer in the place, he picked up the newspaper someone left behind, thought how much it looked like the one he'd just thrown away and sat reading it anyway. Only the prices had changed.

The manager mopped the floor and chewed out a tall woman cleaning the mixer. She had flour on her face and looked ready to cry. When Dray left Biscuit Town, he went to K-Mart, bought one roll of shelf paper with blue squares. He rolled it on a shelf at home, laid a table knife down to hold the edge and cut it with scissors. He did two shelves before he had to go back to K-Mart. This time, he bought eight rolls, all they had in the blue pattern, carried them from the store like a load of firewood. He only used three more. Then he cleaned the lower cabinets, throwing out sticky skillets, warped and brown-stained baking sheets, cake pans, everything.

Under the sink, he pulled out caked boxes of bleach, half-empty bottles of floor wax that had separated into layers, silver polish that had dried to pink pumice. The whole thing smelled like earth under a rock when you rolled it away. In a dark corner something gleamed like a single eye. He knelt to reach it. A glass marble. One of Pete's, probably. Some cereal box premium that had most likely meant a fight between Pete and Iris. The marble was round and cool. He rolled it in his palm. Dray finally dropped it into his shirt pocket. If Pete called tonight he'd tell him about it. But why should he call tonight? It wasn't Christmas or Father's Day.

"You know how it is, Dad," Pete said. "I'm over extended and the company thinks you're rubber. They have your ass in a sling every minute."

Drayton knew how it was ... how it used to be. He had worked when he could have finished up, come on home. And the excuses he used when he didn't want to do anything.

"Daddy has to work." He rubbed it in. With Ree too. Made the guilt go as far as it could. She'd say, "Daddy's tired. He had to work." She'd worked all day too, but somehow he'd never paid much attention to what she did. He thought clothes cleaned themselves, food appeared already on the table, a kitchen was cleaned in minutes. He never noticed.

By ten, when Pete hadn't called, Dray tried to remember the last time the phone rang

... some gimmick giveaway vacation for two if he'd buy into a beach condo. He let the girl give out her whole sales talk. In fact, he kept her on the phone, asking prices and dates, before he finally said he wasn't interested right now but to call again anytime she wanted to.

He called Helen. As the phone rang, he had second thoughts, almost hung up. She might be in bed, but he heard background music as she answered.

"Sorry to be calling so late," he said.

He could tell she didn't know who it was. "Drayton," he said, "Drayton Brewster. You fixed my pants."

"Oh, yes," she said. "They fit okay?"

"Fine," he said, "just fine, couldn't be better. How are you?"

Helen said she thought she might be taking a little cold or it could be hay fever. Certain things bloomed in spring and she had fits of sneezing. If she ever found out what it was, she'd get rid of it in her yard. He said he knew how that was. When he measured laundry detergent, he always spilled some and that made him sneeze.

"Don't measure," she said. "You dump. Like you cook. A pinch of this, pinch of that."

He ended up asking her out Wednesday night, saying he'd pick her up at six.

The next day he cleaned the attic. He threw out hobbyhorses, piled up boxes of fabric, patterns, stuffed animals missing arms, legs, ears, their entrails gray as fog. He stacked up lopsided Christmas wreaths, flattened decorations, boxes of smashed ribbon bows and a basket of used wrapping paper Renita had pressed, refolded. He shoved old furniture from the eaves, called the Blue House, a charity group in town, to pick up. They were out within an hour, had the truck backed across his lawn to the front door.

The door hadn't been opened all winter, and the men had to push from the outside while he pulled. Dray thought the glass was going to break when the door came open with a great jerk. While the men carried out the furniture, their big feet thundering up and down stairs, he quickly grabbed clothes from Renita's closet, shoved them into their arms. "Take these too. They might do somebody some good."

The men waited while he pushed hat boxes at them, handbags, gowns and robes and slippers, brought him plastic bags into which he raked bottles and jars of things from the dresser, emptied drawers of earrings, necklaces, and cheap, glittery pins.

"Mister," one of them said, "you sure you want to get rid of all this? My wife'd kill me if I hauled off her stuff like this. She must have done you awful wrong."

"My wife's dead," Drayton said. "Seven months now."

"Oh, sorry." The man shook his head. "Sorry."

After they left, he took down curtains and blinds, vacuumed the room, washed drawers, left them open to air. He raised the windows and just stood there breathing awhile. Someone had already cut their grass and there was the sharp scent of wild onions in the air. It made him hungry. In the kitchen he fixed an onion and peanut butter sandwich, licked the knife, poured a glass of buttermilk, then sat on the brick back steps to eat. A blue jay mocked him from the tree, walking back and forth on a limb, screaming "Jay. Jay. Jay." It sounded like "Dray. Dray. Dray."

The bread in his sandwich was stale, so he threw it under the tree for the jay. At least that would shut him up for a while. It did.

Dray turned on *The Speeding Light*, napped on the sofa. It was four-thirty when he woke. Wind came from Renita's room,e chased down the hall and chilled him.

He pulled the windows down, shaved and showered, then put on first one shirt then another. Every time he changed shirts, he had to change ties, and that took him a while. By the time he got to the car in the garage, he felt sticky all over, his suit limp. He'd lost so much weight the jacket hung loose on his shoulders, his pants bunched in the back under his belt. He hadn't taken this pair for Helen to alter. Now he wished he had.

Those she fixed fitted him and he felt better wearing them. He just couldn't wear them to church. How would that look at Prayer Meeting? Not that he knew. He hadn't been in more years than he could count, but where else could you go on Wednesday night?

Helen wore a pink dress with a sweater of the same color around her shoulders. Her hair had been freshly done. He smelled spray and sneezed. He held the car door for her and they talked of the weather. She didn't ask where they were going. He just drove, and when they parked in front of church, she seemed surprised but didn't say anything. There were only ten people in the whole sanctuary. All of them stared at Drayton as he led Helen to a pew not too far from the back and not too close to the front either. He thought he heard whispers, but then the organ started. He shared a hymnal with Helen, noticed how small and white her hands were, that she'd moved her wedding band and diamond to her right hand, wore a pearl ring on her left.

He didn't know what he had done with Renita's rings. They'd been in a small envelope the undertaker handed him. He'd shoved it in his pocket, forgot about them. They might have been among that stuff he gave the Blue House today. During prayer, his stomach growled, low at first, then a rumble. He wondered if anyone else heard it, glanced at Helen and she looked amused, slightly embarrassed. He felt in his pocket for a mint, cough drop, anything. All he felt were the square edges of the little envelope that held Renita's rings. So that's where they were. He would have traded them for a package of Lifesavers right now. Helen nudged him gently with her elbow, offered a roll of mints. He took one and his stomach thanked him, got louder, then finally quiet. They sang the last hymn, "Blessed Be the Tie That Binds" and Drayton listened to Helen's sweet bird voice on the high notes.

He didn't sing. Never had. Singing wasn't something he did. Listening was what he did better. Several people shook his hand as he left the church. Helen waved to someone she knew, stopped to talk a few minutes, natural as if she'd been going to that church all her life.

"Come again," the preacher said. "It's nice to see you in the middle of the week."

Drayton realized later he hadn't introduced Helen.

"I'm sorry," he said.

"That was me," Helen said.

"When?" he asked.

"My stomach."

"I thought it was mine," he said. "I forgot to eat supper. That's the first time I ever did that."

"I didn't know we were going to church," Helen said.

"We could stop and get a bite," he said, thinking of the fried chicken places he'd frequented lately, all the chains on hamburger row, but they were greasy, paper-bag-and-box places. It was nearly nine. No real eating place was open.

"Do you know Walt's?" Helen asked.

"You mean Walter Kelly's Drive In? I didn't know he was still in business."

"He makes the best hamburger in town." Helen rolled her window down, let the breeze play in her hair.

"Walt's it is." He aimed the car in that direction, surprised he remembered.

The small green and white store with the drive-in shelter and speakers was still there. A jukebox played inside and Willie Nelson sang something about Texas. Two trucks with teenagers were parked side by side, boys in one, girls the other. They hollered and laughed back and forth, held up blasting radios. Willie now crooned about ribbons in her hair.

After Drayton placed their order, he glanced at Helen, her profile clean and smiling in the light. He leaned back in his seat, stretched his arms above his head and realized he suddenly felt at least a hundred years younger. All at once.

He started to hum as Willie Nelson sang about girls he'd loved in his life. Maybe Drayton didn't sing, but he was a pretty good hummer, and right now that filled in the space with a warm center that seemed to get wider and warmer. Then Helen joined in and by the time their food came they were talking about her daughters and his son and the crafts festival in Martinsville next week. There were onions on Drayton's hamburger. He'd forgotten to say leave them off.

Helen peered into her burger, said, "Oh, onions. Good. I don't think a hamburger is a hamburger without onions."

He knew she was thinking the same thing. And he didn't want to rush things. It was all right. In fact. it was finer than fine. They were both on the same thought train and it was chugging right along. Chugging right along.

The Bridesmaid's Story

Maid of Honor

Maybe it was the wildflowers that attracted Ludeen Hucks, the odd, uninvited, unexpected bridesmaid, the day Cordelia Owens Brafford got married. Cordelia wanted an outdoor wedding, somewhere in a meadow, on a mountaintop. Her parents refused. They couldn't invite their friends. Why, there might be insects and stones and goodness knows, where would people sit? Those awful folding funeral chairs? Never. Not their "Delia." Not their baby, Paige Brafford said.

They wouldn't attend their own daughter's wedding if Delia insisted on such, and in their eyes she would never be married if they weren't there to witness it. They implored Bo's parents, who they'd known since all of them were infants, were closer than family. And Bo had been in and out of their house all these years. Certainly they couldn't accomplish anything in life without the sanctity and blessings of First Church, their own church, where two stained-glass windows bore their names and if truth be known a couple of the cornerstones as well. Cordelia gave in. There would be ten bridesmaids, her cousin Sissy, maid of honor, little Franklin Pierce ring bearer, everything her parents and grandparents wanted. But the flowers. She wanted bouquets of wildflowers, chicory, Queen Anne's lace, daisies, coreopsis.

"Darling," her mother implored, "all white arrangements are much more harmonizing.

"No." Cordelia refused. "Wildflowers or no wedding. We'll run away in the night."

Her mother's heart caught. The shame to even think such a dreadful thing. It simply wasn't done in their family.

"It can be charming," her mother told the florist. "If you keep them as background, never the focal point. Fill in here and there with a touch or two of Queen Anne's Lace, chicory." She almost whispered it. To her friends she said Cordelia had always had so much originality and they certainly wanted this wedding to be what she wanted, down to the last detail. Cordelia and Bo picked every wildflower bordering the golf course, in fields and pastures. They picked buckets, laughing, getting tan, sprinkled with gold-flecked freckles.

"Such fair skin," her mother said. "Delia's always had an extremely delicate complexion." Paige took each freckle as a reckless thwarting of parental guidance.

While Cordelia waited in the dressing room, every freckle glowed. Her face glistened and even her mother's breath warmed in her throat as her daughter stood ready to walk down the aisle. The wedding dress that had been used for two generations had been perfectly refitted. Not a seam showed, not a tuck puckered. Cordelia peered through her grandmother's mantilla. The world looked like a landscape under snow.

The harpist played Pachelbel's *Canon*. Five bridesmaids in blue walked down. Then five more. A dark figure followed. Dark and heavy and slow. Her footsteps heard another music, saw only the flowers. She stopped in front of the altar, gazed at the minister in his black robe, lifted her square wooden face and waited. Ludeen Hucks. The congregation drew a deep audible breath. Of course. She and her mother went to every wedding in town. They sat in the church balcony, the corner, dark and square like boxes or pieces of forgotten furniture.

They always got to church early, before any of the wedding party and, quietly, quickly slipped in. If anyone noticed the odd pair, they assumed the two were to help the caterer or part of the custodial staff. Ludeen and her mother Borne weren't dressed for a wedding. In winter they wore bulky brown or gray coats and headscarves; in summer, faded cotton dresses with low-heeled, sturdy, lace-up shoes. It didn't matter they didn't know the bride or groom or weren't invited to the wedding; they went anyway. To all four of the downtown churches, the fifth, an Episcopalian, didn't have a balcony, no place they could watch and not be seen. But to the red brick Baptist, white-domed Presbyterian, blue-doored Catholic and round Lutheran, the mother, Borne, and daughter, Ludeen, went for every wedding.

Some weekends they went twice. When the bride and groom kissed, Ludeen and Borne looked at each other, smiled and nodded. It was just like TV, only better. And when the church emptied, they went home. Home was a three-room apartment on a back street behind a building that had once been a bakery, but was now an outlet store: Nothing Over $10. On the sidewalk in front of their apartment, the two held a yard sale every Saturday morning, hauling out their sun-faded sign on a stick, setting up a rusted metal folding table they kept year round. They sold what they salvaged in nightly rounds behind stores: parts of old displays, odd decorations, soiled or torn merchandise that Borne had washed and mended, little cloth animals Borne stitched from scraps and Ludeen stuffed with packing materials.

The mother and daughter went after the stores closed at five and before the garbage pickup at six or seven the next morning. They went through things around town piled on curbs for pickup, carted home toys, clothes, baby furniture, outdated lamps and whatever else could be sold. They prowled in the dusk like two stray cats, were as familiar to the town cops as the maple trees on Main Street.

"There's Ludeen and Borne." Frank Grimes tapped his horn and waved. They waved back. But only Ludeen smiled. She smiled most of the time, a wooden, painted-on, doll kind of smile.

She probably slept with that smile on her face. Slept in her small cot pushed against the wall in her mother's bedroom. With the dolls. Those that weren't for sale, and all the bride dolls. Borne at her old treadle sewing machine in the living room. Cut and stitched clothes for the naked dolls she pulled from trashcans, curb piles. Dolls, whose faces had been tattooed with designs in ballpoint pen ink, lipstick, or felt-tip markers. Dolls with dangling arms, twisted legs, unwashed hair and unbathed bodies. Sometimes Ludeen bathed with them, dolls of all sizes surrounding her in the tub, where she sat like a pot roast, potatoes and carrots bobbing all around.

She scrubbed them with brushes and cloths, soap, then powdered and perfumed, let them dry naked as plucked birds in a row on the quilt-covered sofa. Sometimes they put a doll dressed as a bride on the yard sale table, just to hear people exclaim, ask how much? "Not for sale," Borne always said. "I dressed it for my daughter."

At that Ludeen smiled loud, showed all her teeth wide to molars, strong and white, even as pickets on a fence. She laughed in a loud neigh. People expected a whinny to follow. Instead there was silence as the smile stayed stuck. Summers they sold flowers Borne grew every place she could in the yard next to the service station remodeled into a Quick Stop, and next to the concrete wall they added, she planted tall things that grew in shade. Ludeen picked wildflowers, anything that bloomed in yards where a house emptied and went up for sale. Nobody said anything. They only picked flowers. No harm in that. Until the wedding. The harpist played the *Canon* again. Everyone in the wedding looked at each other. Was anyone going to do anything? Who was this person? What was she doing here? The minister caught Owen Sifford Brafford's eye, gave a quick, almost unnoticeable lift with his chin. Cordelia's father took his daughter's arm. The organist sounded her cue. The two walked to the altar. Ludeen stepped closer to the flowers, heard the music for the first time, saw the bride approaching on her father's arm.

The minister began and the ceremony went without incident. Like the bad fairy at the blessing of the princess, Ludeen watched every movement. Her mother stood at the back of the church. She couldn't go after Ludeen, pull her away. It would make a worse scene. All she could do was imagine Ludeen seeing it like a television show.

"Happily ever after," Ludeen said after soap opera weddings. "Happily ever after." Sometimes clapping her hands.

Borne hoped she wouldn't this time. Maybe she'd realize where she was. A little. The minister finished. Bo lifted Cordelia's veil and Ludeen put her hand over her mouth. Borne waited as if she had been carved from wax. Ludeen only smiled. The organ sounded and the bride and groom sped up the aisle, followed by the pattern of attendants. It was like Ludeen wasn't there. Everyone stepped around her, moved according to plan.

Then the crowd surged forward to the vestibule, to the double doors, to the reception, to champagne and a wedding cake seven tiers tall. Borne pressed hard against the wall until the church emptied. Only Ludeen stood at the altar, picking wildflowers from the arrangements. Borne took Ludeen's arm, pulled her toward the aisle. Ludeen gave her a laugh, showed all her teeth, tasted tears for the first time. Her mother wiped them with ribbons from the flowers, patted her hand like an old woman, patted and rubbed her hand as they walked up the aisle, the oddest maids of the party.

The Story of the Banker's Wife

Blackberries

Whenever Joan and Lanelle walked, black women coming to clean houses in the neighborhood waved to them. Behind the steering wheels in their clean, old cars, the maids lifted their hands and waved.

Lanelle smiled. "I bet they wonder what I'm doing here."

Joan didn't know what she meant. She didn't know until after Lanelle moved and Joan walked alone and the maids no longer waved. Then she knew.

Joan met Lanelle walking.

Joan liked to walk early mornings, when everything was quiet, when people were still in bed or reading papers or dawdling over breakfast. She rarely met anyone when she walked.

Until she met Lanelle walking her dog, a Sheltie, Roby, who pranced on the end of his leash, whined to be let loose, pleaded with eyes that promised, I'll be good. Honest. I'll come back when you call. Just let me run a little. Usually, at least, once a week, Lanelle let Roby run and sniff on a vacant lot or drink from the creek.

She and Joan waited and talked while the dog had his run. Sometimes they walked ahead and let him catch up with them. Lanelle made sure he stayed in sight.

Lanelle was taller than Joan, wore khaki shorts, t-shirts, and sandals. She had a tangle of long dark hair she pulled back. Tanned, she had a sprinkle of freckles and unusual eyes: one blue, one brown. Joan noticed right away. She'd never known anyone whose eyes didn't match.

Lanelle laughed. "Most people don't notice. I'm glad you did."

"Sorry," Joan said. "I didn't mean to stare, but ..."

"You didn't," Lanelle said. "You paused a moment and I caught it. Just a flicker that told me you noticed. It's one of the things I get a kick out of watching when I meet somebody. If they don't notice right away, I wonder how long it will take and if they'll say anything."

Lanelle introduced herself, reached out to shake hands, which startled Joan. This was the most informal of settings. Maybe it was an automatic gesture with Lanelle.

Joan introduced herself, shook Lanelle's hand. "I live up on Fountaine," she said. "Three streets over. Do you walk every day?"

"Several times. But not usually long walks. Just around the block or so to take Roby out," Lanelle said.

Joan walked almost two miles. She'd measured it with the car odometer.

Lanelle began to walk the two miles with her. Sometimes she left the dog at home. "He stops too much and I get impatient with him." But usually Roby walked too. "Mexico is the place never to take dogs. Don't ever take your dogs to Mexico," she said, not long after she and Joan started walking together. "Even if you make sure they drink bottled water, they get stuff.

They get sick and you can't find a vet. If we ever go to Mexico again, the dogs stay home."

Lanelle's other dog was so old he only walked as far as the end of the drive, then wagged his tail but didn't try to follow. Bob's muzzle was white and he limped badly, walked with a slow hitch. He also wore a tiny bottle tied with string on the end of his tail.

Lanelle explained Bob didn't hold his tail up. He let it drag and all the fur had worn off. His tail stayed sore until she started to put on the plastic bottle when he went out. Bob whined when they left him.

One day as they left him in the driveway, there was a yip and a flash of fur and screams. "Damn him," Lanelle said and handed Roby's leash to Joan. "He's half dead until that cat next door comes out. Then he chases her."

The cat sat on the porch roof like a large white bird licking herself. Lanelle grabbed Bob by the collar, scolded him. "Bad dog, bad dog. You know not to do that." She tugged him home, locked him inside.

"There's something about that cat that sets him off. Of all the cats in the neighborhood to chase, it has to be that one." She shook Roby's leash. "Those people don't like us. They've complained once and threatened to call the pound if Bob chases their cat again."

Lanelle lived in a small rental house on a short side street tucked between two new housing developments. It was an old street with trees almost bigger than the dozen or so houses, three of which were rented.

"We signed the lease for ninety days," Lanelle said. "We're looking for a house to buy ... if we decide to stay on this coast."

Lanelle, her husband, Jack, and the two dogs came to the South from the West Coast by way of Mexico. They had spent six months on the Baja Peninsula traveling and living in a huge pink and white recreational vehicle. It was as big as a bus.

"I bet the neighbors don't exactly like the idea of that thing parked on the street," Lanelle said. The "bus" was too big to go in the driveway. It had Mexico license plates and was plastered with travel stickers from places Joan could not pronounce.

"Why here?" Joan asked. The neighborhood was nice enough, but the town was small and Lanelle said her husband painted. She didn't say he was an artist, only that he painted and had taken some art classes. In what sounded like a fit of midlife crisis, they quit good jobs in Seattle, sold their house, bought the RV and headed to Mexico for the winter, then to Middleton.

"There are no art galleries here," Joan said. "No tourists. No market for art." She had grown up in Middleton, gone to college, married and moved back.

"I grew up in Montgomery County," Lanelle said. "My mama still lives there. I'd like to be close to her."

"That's wonderful," Joan said. "Have you seen any houses you're interested in?"

"I've seen some we're not interested in. And some real estate agents I'd like to report." Lanelle's voice had a bitter edge.

They walked up one of the nicer streets in the section. Lanelle asked Joan about the people who lived here; what they did for a living?

Joan pointed out a couple of doctors, a dentist, a minister, the CEO of a national corporation, the school superintendent, a banker. The houses tended to be brick, two storied, with basements and double or triple garages. They sported nicely kept lawns that flew flags emblazoned with golf symbols or dogwood blossoms, autumn foliage, pumpkins or witches in the fall. Houses that looked smug and bored and tightly closed, as though they were self-contained and keeping it that way.

"How do you know them?" Lanelle asked.

"From church, that kind of thing," Joan said. "Not socially."

"Are any of them black?"

"I haven't thought about it," Joan said. "I don't know." The people on Joan's street were teachers or school principals, owners of small businesses, typical middle class. Middle class. The first time Joan realized it, she laughed. She'd finally made it. The great middle class. Once in elementary school, when she was doing social studies homework in something like the fourth or fifth grade, she remembered asking her mother, "Are we lower, middle or upper class?"

Her mother stood behind the ironing board, ironing one garment after another. It seemed her mother was always ironing. Joan associated the smell of warm, clean clothes with her mother.

Her mother paused a minute, unrolled a starched blouse that had been sprinkled with water from the tin nippled Pepsi bottle, said, "Oh, put us down as middle."

Joan had. She didn't know until she took Intro to Sociology that they were lower class. She'd always thought lower class meant very poor and poor people were dirty, lived in houses without screens and wore clothes without buttons. Her family wore clean clothes, lived in a clean house that had screens. Their neighbors did too. Their house was the only rented house in the neighborhood. The Lowders who owned it only had it painted once. That was when they furnished the paint and Joan's father painted it. Her father tried to get them to do it the next time it needed painting and they refused. Joan's family replaced the screens, put down new kitchen flooring and painted the rooms inside.

"I hate fixing up somebody else's house," her mother said often, "but I won't live in a mess."

The street Joan and Lanelle walked was a few notches up in the middle. Upper middle, she guessed. No blacks she knew of. Though there had been one family a few years ago, several streets over. They had been transferred in by the paper company and only stayed a year.

Joan heard gossip that the real estate agent who sold the blacks that house later lost her license. Other agents blacklisted her. Rumor was she was set up in some shady deal and got left holding the bag. She had to turn her business over to her partner, stay in the office and handle finances. She couldn't sell anymore.

"What did they do? The real estate agents?"

"It's not what they did," Lanelle said, "it's the things they said and tone of voice. Not anything you can prove."

"Prove?" Why would you want to prove anything? Joan thought.

"Race," Lanelle said. "I don't like the way they bring that up."

"How?"

"We were looking at this one house, in a fairly nice section and the agent said, 'One thing's for sure. You won't have any blacks living here.'" Lanelle let Roby off his leash and he sniffed a healthy boxwood that lined the walk of a white brick two-story house. "If we bought a house, I sure wouldn't buy from him."

Joan couldn't remember anything a real estate agent ever said to them that constituted a racial slur and they had bought and sold several houses. Maybe she just hadn't been aware of it. Tuned in. The house they had now was one of the oldest in the section and neglected. They had gotten it for a good price, then slowly and gradually refurbished it, done the work themselves, from refinishing floors to tearing out walls.

Joan and Lanelle walked to a cul-de-sac and a long, cream-colored brick house where they turned around and started back. Joan had measured this way once in her car and clocked off where a mile ended; that way she made sure she got in a two-mile walk every day. Lanelle took her word for it. And Roby had gotten so he knew the route, where they turned, where there was a vacant lot or woods coming up and he waited to lift his leg there, to let loose his yellow dribble.

The banker's house always looked so perfectly kept you'd swear no one lived there. It was a magazine picture. Joan imagined its cream-colored carpet, silk flowers, and polished furniture. From the outside she saw how folds in draperies hung equal distance apart and each valence looked as proper as a top hat. The yard stayed groomed, each blade of grass knew what was expected of it and did it. There were no weeds. Landscaping looked buttoned in place.

Just beyond the banker's green lawn grew a patch of tangled blackberry vines. A tall wall of a thicket. It grew near the power towers. Joan thought at first it was odd the banker's house was so near the power lines, then she realized, this was the highest hill for miles, the best view. Every morning in July while the blackberries were ripe, Joan picked two or three. Their wild taste on her tongue made her remember as a child how her mother picked blackberries for their breakfast cereal. Or a cobbler. A blackberry cobbler was still Joan's idea of Heaven. Here, there was never enough to even think cobbler and even if there had been, Joan would never have picked that many without asking permission from someone. Probably the power company.

She had to urge Lanelle to taste a blackberry. Lanelle had tasted blackberries before, but they were always in a pie or sweetened with cream. It took her several mornings to taste the real blackberry flavor without sugar. Roby liked them from the start. He got a berry or two from each of them, chewed as they walked.

"They're full of vitamin C," Joan told Lanelle to get her to try them.

Lanelle was health conscious. That was one of the reasons she was now thinking of not staying here, near her family. "We're too different. They eat fried foods. Everything has to be fried."

"Everything?" Joan asked.

"All the Southern stuff."

"But you grew up Southern," Joan said. "Are you saying you've changed and they haven't and you don't have much in common anymore?"

"That's exactly what I'm saying," Lanelle replied.

Lanelle had grown up in the Allen community in the next county, she said once. They had no running water and the whole community shared a well, but she had gone to school at Duke. On a scholarship, she explained to Joan. Then got accepted into a graduate school in California, married, divorced and John was her second husband. Joan asked once how they met and Lanelle laughed, hesitated, and then finally said they met in a bar. She'd been embarrassed to say it. She didn't go to bars, but she had been on vacation, alone, in a small town on an island in Puget Sound, staying in a tiny hotel. It was just after her divorce, she couldn't sleep, so she dressed and went across the street to the bar, sat down at the only empty seat in the place and it turned out to be next to John, who was going through his first divorce. It was love at first sight.

"And the rest is ..."

Joan waited for her to say "history."

"... us," Lanelle said.

Joan moaned to Lanelle of the bad haircut she'd gotten the day before. Really bad. Joan even wore a hat to walk. "Till I can get to another shop to get something done," she told Lanelle.

"I know what you mean," Lanelle said. "I don't let just anyone cut my hair. Don't you check out the person before you let them cut?"

"Not nearly enough," Joan muttered and pulled down her hat with both hands.

"I have regular hair," Lanelle said. "And if I don't get the right cut, I get a mess."

"What's regular hair?" Joan asked.

"What I have," said Lanelle. "Like this." She fluffed her dark, wavy hair.

"Like mine," Joan said. "Except I have a perm and yours is natural."

"I got my father's hair," Lanelle said. "When I was growing up, I got razzed all the time about my hair."

"It's beautiful."

Another day Lanelle again mentioned her father. "He was white."

Okay, Joan thought. What's the big deal? Mine was too.

"My mother is black," Lanelle said.

"Oh," Joan said.

"I grew up in the black community," Lanelle said, "but all my life I've passed for white."

"I thought you were tanned," Joan said. "You looked tanned to me. From Mexico."

"I'm tanned all the time," Lanelle said and pinched the flesh of her upper arm. "This is my color year round."

Joan didn't know what to say. This was her friend and she was still the same person she was two minutes ago, two weeks ago, a month ago when Joan met her.

"My mother was married to a black man who raised me, but my biological father was white. He raped her."

"Oh," Joan said again. She didn't know what else to say. "Did you know him?" she asked. "Your ... blood father?"

"I knew him, but he didn't know me," Lanelle said. "Or he never acted like he did. My mother said she told him, but he never acknowledged it. Never helped her out any. The man I called daddy, who married my mother, was a wonderful father to me. Never raised his hand to me. He died when I was twelve." Lanelle continued walking, telling her story. "I was living with a white woman then. She took me in to stay with her, sent me to school. Mother sent word my daddy was sick and for me to come and Mrs. Howell wouldn't take me to see him. We had a big fight. She said he wasn't that sick. He was in the hospital. All she could think about was the last time she'd let me go home, when I came back, and unpacked my suitcase, a roach ran out." Lanelle stopped to let the dog off his leash.

Joan waited.

Lanelle laughed. "Mrs. Howell, she screamed, made me wash all my clothes ... my mother had already washed and ironed them. I had to do them all again. I've never seen a woman so scared of a little bitty bug."

Joan hurt for the twelve-year-old Lanelle had been. She wanted to hug her friend. Joan wanted to say I'm sorry the woman who was mean to you was white and I am white, that she did this to you. They kept walking.

"Did you hate her?" Joan asked. "After that?"

"No, I didn't ever hate her. She was who she was and old and kind to me in her way. I went to the funeral."

"Her funeral?"

"My daddy's funeral. She took me to that."

"Well, that was the least," Joan said, furious now at the woman. "That was too late."

"I forgave her," Lanelle said. "I had to grow up some to do it, but I worked through it. She sent me to Duke."

"But you had to have had the grades to get in," Joan said. "You did that yourself."

"Then graduate school got me as far away from Mrs. Howell and my family as I could go, without landing in the ocean." Lanelle laughed. She had beautiful teeth, and a good smile. An open smile.

"It was easier to pass in California," she said.

"Pass?"

"Pass for white," Lanelle said. "I'm doing it now."

"All this time," Joan said. She laughed.

"All this time, you looked tanned to me."

When they came to the blackberry patch, it had been picked clean.

"End of the season," Joan said.

"Just when I finally got used to eating them without sugar." Lanelle laughed again.

As they turned the corner, a cream-colored car came from the garage at the banker's house.

Mrs. Banker buzzed down her window and said something Joan didn't understand, then shot off in a sharp puff of diesel exhaust.

"That didn't sound friendly," Lanelle said.

"She's not a friendly person," Joan said. She told Lanelle about the banker's first wife, whom everybody loved, how she died suddenly and the banker was desolate. This woman had a hard, pinched look and a screech for a voice. People who knew the banker said he was better off in his loneliness and grief. At least it was quiet. There was no pleasing his wife. At church Joan heard people on committees say they couldn't work with her and if the man stayed married to her a year, he was a candidate for sainthood.

Joan wondered if she ought to measure out another walking route. Maybe the banker's wife didn't want walkers on her street.

"Maybe it's me," Lanelle said. "She knows I'm black."

"She can't," Joan said. "I didn't and I'm closer to you than she has ever been."

"The maids know," Lanelle said.

Early mornings at the end of September had a chill and a bit of a bite to them. Sometimes Joan wore a light windbreaker when she walked, Lanelle a khaki jacket. She had packed everything else.

Furniture Lanelle and John had used for three months was given to her mother.

They ran a classified ad to sell the refrigerator. There was not a lot to pack in the RV or car. She'd drive the car cross country with one dog. John would take the RV and the other dog. He left first.

The last morning Joan walked with Lanelle. When they came to where the blackberry vines had been, there was only a bare spot. A clean, pale place on the ground. All the vines had been cut down. Somebody had whacked them and kept cutting them down until they were low enough to mow.

Above, the power tower loomed large and empty. It was steely silver and strong.

"That's odd," Joan said. Nothing else in the area had been mowed.

"Somebody didn't want us eating their blackberries," Lanelle said.

As Joan left Lanelle the last time, she zipped up her jacket, turned around and waved. Roby barked.

"I'll keep in touch,"Lanelle said.

"Promise," Joan said. "Send me your new address as soon as you have one. Who knows? I may get to the West Coast one of these days."

"I'll leave the light on," Lanelle said. She waved.

Weeks later at the grocery store, the banker's wife wheeled her cart past Joan, then on impulse, whipped it around, came back and said, "Those were our blackberries, you know. They were on our land. We enjoyed them."

Joan didn't know what to say. That must have been what the banker's wife said that day from her car window. Joan had assumed because the area was so wild and the banker's lawn so well kept, the land belonged to the power company. Or nobody. There had certainly been enough berries to share. The area was large as a good-sized tool shed and she and Lanelle only picked five or six each daily. Plus the two or three for the dog. There always seemed to be berries left. The bushes weren't loaded but there always seemed to be plenty.

"I didn't know," Joan told Mrs. Banker. "I had no idea they were yours." She didn't say she was sorry, because she wasn't. She was only sorry the bushes had been destroyed. She was sorry her friend had moved so far away. And she was sorry the maids when they drove past her in the mornings no longer waved.

The Lady Professor's Story: Part I

The deer was, then wasn't. A quick blur, a shape in her headlights, then a hard muffled thud. Andrea swerved her car in the wall of sudden dark and stopped beside the road. The deer was gone. Had she only imagined it? Had she imagined too, the sound? Andrea took the flashlight from the glove compartment, flicked it on and felt better. She eased into the wet grass toward the ditch, following the narrow yellow ribbon her flashlight made. The light caught antlers tangled like shrub in the ditch. A deer, the color of dead leaves, lay still as a stone. In the silence she imagined she heard its heart race like a motor trying to catch up, then slow and get slower still until it quit and there was only the dark stillness and recently stopped rain dripping softly from leaves. The rain had been hard and fast and came down in sheets. Andrea had concentrated on that when she realized she had run out of the rain and something else had shot across the road in front of her.

There wasn't another car in sight. She didn't know what to do. Drive away and pretend it never happened? She'd seen deer dead by the road several times, watched their bodies swell, bloat and finally blend with the earth and leaves. She didn't want to do that. Ahead she saw a lighted building. She got back into the car and cranked it, gave it the gas and nothing happened. She checked the brake, which was off, gave the car more gas and still it would not go forward. She heard a metal scrape when she tried to back, but the car would not go backwards either. She got out, and with her flashlight saw a badly dented front fender that wouldn't allow the right tire to turn. Damn, she thought, and got back in and cut the engine.

Andrea walked in the wet roadside weeds toward the little lighted building. Her shoes would be ruined. She walked on the paved road in the mist, glad of her raincoat and that she didn't need an umbrella. Carrying the flashlight and her purse was enough. Had she locked the car? Yes, when she got her purse. A woman alone on a road at night had to be careful. Who knows what might leap out of the woods?

The volunteer fire station had several vehicles parked in front of it. Mostly pick-up trucks with gun racks and bumper stickers that said things like "Forget Hell" or "Get Right With God." If she hadn't known better she would have thought it was a Honky Tonk, a poolhall, a beer den.

When she opened the door, the men sitting around a small black and white TV looked surprised, caught by a woman. Talk stopped. Half a laugh hung in midair.

"Whoa here," one of the men said. "What can we do for you this time of night, little lady?"

"I hit a deer," she said. "I think I killed it." Why did her voice suddenly sound as if she were about to cry?

The men laughed. "Cussed things. They dart out before you know it. Before you can stop. Wrecked many a car."

There was a chorus of agreement and somebody in the back started their own deer-killing story.

Andrea thought all the room lacked was a pot-bellied stove with a blue speckled coffee pot burbling atop it. Instead they sat around a flickering TV that sang and danced beer commercials.

"Let's see what we can do about all this." One man unfolded himself from a chair and stretched toward a phone on the wall. "Carl's gonna hate coming out on a night like this."

"Ah, let'im do something to earn his keep," one of the men said. The others laughed.

Andrea stood by the door while the man made the call. Someone held up a Styrofoam cup, asked, "Coffee?"

She shook her head no.

Several men shrugged into their raincoats, pulled on boots.

Didn't they know the rain had stopped, or were they just being prepared because they were firemen? Andrea wondered.

They followed her out and two of the men insisted she ride with them. They got in, but one held the door for her.

There were tools on the floor of the truck and greasy rags, fast food wrappers, blue and yellow parts of plastic toys. It smelled of peanut butter and apple cores.

"You ever think about cleaning up your truck?" the fireman beside her asked the driver.

"Shoot," the driver said. "My truck's clean.

1. This uns my wife's."

They drove past her car, then turned and parked facing it, got out and left the headlights on. One of the men stepped down into the ditch beside the deer, held up its head. "It's dead all right."

The other truck stopped behind her and the rest of the men waited for Carl, who came quicker than she expected. His truck had a red light on the dash.

"I was down the bridge when the call came in."

"We thought we'd give you one more thing to do before you called it a night," the fireman who gave Andrea the ride said. "Cap the night off right."

Andrea noticed Carl's brown uniform had an official looking patch at his shoulder and he carried a clipboard. He examined the deer. "Eight pointer. See any others?"

Andrea said, "No," and shivered.

"Stag night?" one of the men said and the others laughed.

She wondered what happened now.

"Good hundred fifty pounds," Carl said. "You want it?"

"Me?" Andrea said. "No, I couldn't." What would anyone want with a dead deer? A hundred pounds of dead meat.

"Why not?" one of the men said. "Good eating. They don't turn up their nose at anything at my house. The way grocery prices are these days."

She thought of her neighbors. The father was either out of work or didn't work at all. The mother, who always looked sad eyed and tired, sewed in a curtain factory. There were three little girls who the mother said ate deer and thought it was steak. "It's the only meat we ever have," she told Andrea once. "Deer stew, ground deer, roast. You get used to it." She said her husband shot and skinned several a year. The husband, Andrea had heard, trapped animals and sold their furs. Andrea had forgotten this could be a way to earn a living. And the animal fur business must be down lately because of all the protests. She couldn't wear animal skins and she couldn't eat their bodies. But the deer was dead and would be hauled away to a landfill.

"Could I give it to someone?" she asked.

"After I fill out these forms and you sign them, it's your deer," Carl said as he scribbled on his clipboard. He propped his knee on the fender of her car and wrote using a small penlight held close to the page.

"My neighbor hunts," she said. If she gave them this deer that was already dead, it would save another one from being killed to stock the freezer this winter. "I'll call Ken as soon as I get home."

"Ken Busby?" one of the men asked. "I know him. This deer's more than Ken's bagged the last couple of years. Guess he'd do better if he used a car instead of a gun."

He offered to call Ken on his phone.

Andrea waited until the call was finished and the man came back. "Ken said tell you much obliged." To the game warden he turned and said, "We got him out of bed, but he said for that much meat, he'd be down as soon as he got his pants on. Plans to skin it tonight, dress it out."

The men put a tire tool behind Andrea's fender and three of them pushed on it until the metal gave a mighty pop and looked convex again. "Now see if you can't move it, little lady," one of them said.

This time the car moved forward. She rolled down her window and thanked them. They were as jovial as if they've been on a hunt. They'd had an adventure. Her deer hit and her car would be conversation the rest of the evening, leading into the other deer hits and fender- bender stories.

As Andrea drove home, she thought of those three little girls through the winter eating thick brown stews and sandwiches piled high with slices of deer roast. She'd take her bean soup. Bean soup didn't leap into your sleep.

When she switched on the bedroom lamp, her husband said, "What took you so long?"

"I hit a deer."

"Why didn't you just come on home?" he asked. "You didn't brand it."

She didn't try to explain, just brushed her teeth, washed her face and changed into plaid flannel pajamas that felt like home to her skin and smelled like last night's sleep. Her husband hated her sense of responsibility. "You think the world spins on your little finger and if you let go for a second, the whole thing would come crashing down."

She tried to tell him that wherever she was she made her little corner of the world and she wanted to keep it as clean of guilt as she could sweep it.

"Come to bed," he said, and turned toward the wall. "I'm tired."

That night she woke to a sound like something blowing their breath outside her window. She raised onto her elbow and in the moonlight saw a huge deer brush his antlers against her screen, then stamp his hooves and bound across the hill behind the house. He stood silhouetted against the moon that had come out full from behind the scudding gray clouds. The deer lifted his head as though he called out a sound that was both mournful and low. A sound she thought she'd heard before but wasn't sure. She wasn't sure she heard anything at all but the silence and her husband's breathing. When she looked again, nothing moved but the moon.

The Lady Professor's Story: Part II

A Fox at Midnight

"Get in the car," her husband said.

He startled Andrea, over the sound of filling the pot.

"Now?" she asked. It was nearly midnight and she still had papers to grade.

He had been out of town for a job interview five hours away.

"Now?" she repeated. "Why?"

She wiped her hands on her jeans, looked at her floppy red bedroom shoes. "I'd have to change."

"No," he said, "grab a coat and come on."

He stood in the doorway. "If you don't hurry, it'll be gone."

"What will be gone?" she asked.

"If I tell you, it won't be any fun."

She tied her shoes. She thought he'd forgotten the word "fun." She couldn't remember the last time she'd heard him use it. Fun. What was fun?"

They drove through woods, around curves, down to the paved road and then the highway toward the river. She was too tired to try to imagine what he wanted to show her. Probably a snake. Sometimes they saw black snakes that stretched half way across the road. In the past they had seen rattlesnakes and copperheads. They could run over a snake, feel it beneath the wheels and look back only to see it whipping crookedly away.

"It's just up ahead," he said.

She thought car wreck. A lost boat that slid from somebody's trailer? Something freakish turned over or pushed up from a thunderstorm?

His car was warm and his briefcase neat on the seat between them.

The highway was leaf spattered from the rain earlier and there was no traffic. There was not a lot of traffic anytime, but even less this late at night. Andrea didn't want to be stranded on this road, or any road, late at night.

"I was grading papers," she reminded him. Then asked herself if she had turned the coffeemaker on or off or unplugged it. She was sure she had not unplugged it. Would she sleep when she finally got to bed in spite of the coffee? She had thought he might stay away overnight. In a motel, not drive home. But when he hadn't called before ten she should have expected him.

"Almost there," he said peering, intently into the dark. "Thought it was about here."

He braked, then turned around in the middle of the road so fast she was thrown against the side. "A U turn on the highway?"

"Why not?" he said. "There's nothing coming."

He got out of the car. "It's still there."

"What?" she asked, seeing nothing. What could he be so excited about? The interview must have gone well and carried him over into this mood. The last six months he'd been so depressed. Several times in the last year she had suggested he see someone.

"Who?" he shouted back at her every time she mentioned it. "Who the hell do you think has all the answers?"

"Talk to a job counselor," she said. "A doctor."

"Ha." He laughed. "You think they whip out a prescription and just like that, snap your fingers, everything will be all right in the world. Why do you think the past is called the past? Because it's past." He had sneered at her, his face dark and twisted.

Now his profile looked straight ahead. He leaned forward, excited. But she saw nothing. Nothing but road, woods, and the air was biting cold. She pulled her sweatshirt close, wished it had a hood. Wished she'd put on a coat.

"There," he said and focused the flashlight on something in the weeds.

Dog? Deer? She hit a deer a year or so ago.

"It's a fox," he said. "See." He moved the light across something orange red, glowing like coals.

"You didn't hit it, did you?" she asked.

"No," he said. "I saw it soon after it was hit though. Stopped and pulled it over to the side of the road."

She reached down and rubbed fur she imagined coarse but so soft she sucked in her breath. It was still warm, or did she only imagine it?

"It's beautiful," she said. A light wind ruffled the red fur. She imagined moist breath steaming slightly from its gently parted mouth.

"It's a female," he said.

"Oh," she said. There were small white pickets of teeth and a black leather nose. Its paws were black partway up the leg like boots. Black boots. She lifted a leg. "Where were you going, lady fox?"

She turned to her husband. "What do we do now?"

He handed her the flashlight, stood with both hands in his pockets. "I don't know. Go home I guess."

"Leave her here? Alone?" Andrea didn't want to leave the fox beside the road.

It started to rain harder and she felt her hair getting wet. She felt the rain's cold fingers on her forehead.

"No," she said.

"No? No? What the hell else can we do?" he asked.

"Bury her," Andrea said. "Take her home and bury her."

"In the dark?" He opened the car door, got in. "Come on."

"I'm not leaving her here."

"Stay then. I'm not burying it." He started the car.

She picked up the dead fox, who felt light as a newborn in her arms. She'd walk back to the house carrying the fox if she had to, but she wasn't leaving it here.

He opened the door on her side. "Get in." Andrea cradled the dead fox all the way home, her wet hair dripping onto it like slow tears. When they got home, he got out of the car but she stayed behind, stroking the soft fur. It was all she could do not to lift the fox and hold her to her shoulder.

"You know, that thing could have rabies," he said as he opened her door.

"No," she said. "It looks too healthy. It's too beautiful." But she stopped stroking the fox and shivered for the first time. Shivered against the rain that had dampened her sweatshirt and the night air.

"Let it go." He took the fox from her and carried it to the porch. "Tomorrow you can call Ken. He can have the fur. Unless you want it. Have him work it up for you?"

"Me?" she said and brushed herself off. "Why would I want it?"

"To wear," he answered.

"No." She shook herself. "Absolutely not." But she didn't want it buried either. The fur gave off a glow of light as though it might still be alive, though she knew it wasn't.

And even if it was late, she called Ken when she went in.

Ken was down there in minutes, boots unlaced, fatigue jacket thrown on, shirt spilling out of his pants.

He shook his head looking at the fox. "She's a beauty. Not a mark on her." He turned the fox over, rubbed her fur between his fingers like a merchant, testing it. Not stroking it as Andrea had done.

"Sure you don't want her?" he said finally, more like a statement than anything else and when Andrea again said, "No," he slung the dead fox over his shoulder and got into his jeep. He was gone as quickly as he came, not gunning his motor as he usually did when he took the hill in front of their house, but quietly stealing away.

Andrea's arms felt empty. She wanted to cry and later, instead of taking a shower before bed, she kept the wild smell of the fox circling her. A small musky smell that she felt followed her for days and she caught people looking at her oddly, as though she knew something she couldn't tell them.

The Lady Professor's Story: Part III

A Snake in the Bush

The first thing she did when she got home was shed clothes, whatever came off quickly and easiest. Unbuttoning, zipping, whatever to get into Herself again. Then she reached for the mail, touching the vital links to friends, family. She got letters. Lots of letters. She wrote letters. She hated the phone. Words in the air were gone. Words on paper were more real than a voice.

She passed her husband on her way in. He didn't look up. He was in the den reading. Since he lost his job he read a lot. Read everything but the classified ads. Sometimes she felt like shoving that section in front of his face, shaking the newspaper to get his attention. To see if there was really anybody inside that shell he seemed to walk around in. She circled some ads in black marker and left them beside his plate. Untouched. Left them several days before she threw the newspaper in the trash, creased as crisply as when she folded it. She felt like rolling up the paper and hitting him, like you do when you train a puppy for soiling the carpet. He was soiling her life ... their life.

She was undressing the rest of the way when he came to the bedroom, stood in the doorway. She pulled on jeans, hung up her hated business suit, the armor that girded her loins daily. She said she'd had a hell of a day, then started into detail.

"Something's going on and I don't like it. Whiff of it. People gave off sparks like rubbing two pieces of flint together. You can see them and if you get too close, you get your fingers, or more, burned."

He said he wrote some letters to some contacts. She thought he was perfectly happy. He had his books, his dog, his hearth. Except the dog was not supposed to be in and she knew he was. She smelled it every day when she came in. And the cat, who was supposed to be an indoor cat, was always outside and met her at the door full of complaints.

She was like Little Red Riding Hood out where wolves lurked in the woods. For years she had wanted to move. The house was cold. Except for the bedrooms, which were too warm to let you sleep well except in the mildest of weather. And the fireplace left your backside cold. They had to buy wood. She'd never forgotten the look on the man's face when he delivered their last load of firewood. "You didn't need this, lady. You got trees." The man opened his arms, gestured around them as though she had never looked. "Crazy," he said and walked back to his truck shaking his head.

She wanted the trees cut, he didn't. He hated yard work of any sort. Out here there was no grass, only ground cover and brush. The last time he cut brush, he'd piddled all day, hacked at saplings hardly bigger than your thumb, then piled them into a heap beside the driveway so she'd be sure to be reminded of his great sacrifice. His monumental effort at outdoor work, making this mountain.

Back in the kitchen, he stood, hands in pockets. "You didn't see."

"See what?"

"My day." He smiled.

How could she *see* his day? There was certainly no evidence of food being prepared for *her* homecoming. But then there rarely was. Unless she fixed it before she left in the mornings, let it cook all day. Dishes from last night's dinner teetered in the sink, topped by his from lunch.

I *see* you haven't done a damn thing all day, she wanted to scream, but didn't. "What?" She looked around.

He seemed to find that amusing and smiled with the corners of his mouth. "Not here."

"Where?" All she saw was what she left this morning plus the mess of the mail on the table.

"Not in here." He smiled. "Outside. I don't see how you missed it."

She did. She was so tired every day she aimed herself for the door and hurled herself in. Now he wanted to play games.

"So," she said. Was it really that big a deal? Nothing had smacked her in the face. The roof was still on. The porch trim still flaked and peeled. Maybe he'd finally gotten around to painting or repairing something. She opened the refrigerator door and peered inside for something unusual. "Is it something that's going to go away?" she asked.

"Not hardly." He smiled and then laughed.

He actually laughed. The sound startled her. How long had it been since she'd heard him laugh? It was one of the things she'd always liked about him.

"Okay." She shut the refrigerator door. "I'm too tired to play Hide and Seek, Guess My Day. What is it? Just tell me."

"I can't tell you. You have to *see* it."

"You *can* tell me," she said. She didn't have time for this. Instead of gritting her teeth, she gripped the edge of the counter with both hands.

"Come on." He reached for her hand. She pulled back. He shrugged, turned and started out. She followed. Reluctantly. This had better be worth it.

He stopped at the driveway, waited. She didn't see anything. She waited for him to go on.

"What?" she said. "For God's sake, what is it?"

He didn't answer.

Then she saw it. Saw the most monstrous snake stretched across the driveway. The snake reached almost from one side of the drive to the other and the body of it was round and thick as an arm. She shivered. She wrapped her arms around herself and shook.

"Don't worry," he said. "It's dead."

"How?" she said. "Where? What?"

"I killed it," he said.

She shivered again and waited for him to go on.

"The cat ..." he said.

"My cat?"

"Your cat kept going toward the brush pile like there was something in it."

The brush pile he had cut last fall and left beside the driveway.

"I heard it," he said. "Heard the rattle every time the cat got close. When the cat backed away, the sound stopped."

She always wondered if she'd know the sound of a rattlesnake if she heard it.

"So I poked a rake in it and the thing uncoiled. Then I got a gun and shot it."

She had forgotten they had a gun. His father's gun. When he settled the estate last year, one of the things he kept was his father's rifle. She didn't even know where it was or if they had bullets that fit it. Obviously he did.

"What do you do with it now?" she asked.

He shrugged his shoulders, said, "Beats me. Killing it was enough."

The snake was beautiful in an evil way. She studied the markings, black and gray diamonds that marched in a row down the snake's back. "Don't people wear these things?"

"The skin?" he asked. "I guess so. If you're so inclined." He was through with the snake. She couldn't take her eyes off it.

"Busbee," she said. "I bet he skins and cures these things."

She called Busbee's and left a message with one of his little girls. "Tell your father we have a snake for him." Once before Busbee had caught a snake in their driveway, a king snake. He saw it, stopped his Jeep and with a stick coaxed the snake into a burlap sack, then tied the top with twine. "These babies," Busbee said, "I'd like to have at my house. They keep the bad ones away."

Maybe if they had kept the king snake he would have kept this bad snake away.

It was nearly dark when Busbee's Jeep came up their drive. Her husband was in the shower. She turned on the floodlights, stood on the deck and heard Busbee let out a whistle when he saw the snake. "Lord a'mighty, this thing could have killed us all. And it's a wonder he hadn't."

He picked the snake up by the rattles, held it aloft, its head dangled close to the ground. "Some piece of work for somebody."

"It's yours," she said.

"Good looking belt," he said. "After it's worked up. Sure you don't want it?"

"Never." She shuddered. "Not for a minute."

"They're pretty things all skinned out."

"Not to me," she answered.

He shook his head as if to say there were all kinds in this world and he was glad he wasn't one of hers. At his Jeep, he threw the snake on the backseat, then holding the door, turned to her and said, "You don't have to keep doing this."

"What?" she asked. "Doing what?"

"You know. Giving me the deer, then that fox ... I thought at first you was setting me up. Now this. We're getting by. We ain't starving." He rubbed his beard. "You can't buy back what you did, if that's what you're trying to do."

She didn't know what to say.

"Setting the law on me wasn't the first time."

"What do you mean? Setting the law on " you."

"They said you did it. Reported my traps."

"No," she said. "I didn't report you. Why would I report you?" Her husband had found the traps along their creek. The dog had been caught in one, her foot only bruised, but her husband had ranted for days. He had reported Busbee.

"Cause you love animals." He spat on the ground. "That don't mean you own them."

"No," she said. "Of course not. But I didn't report you."

"Trial cost me $200, lawyer that much more, but I kept my hunting license."

"I didn't know," she said.

"Sure you did," Busbee said. "A thousand ways."

He slammed his door and with a deafening roar was gone.

She hadn't known. She truly had not known. And yet, Busbee was right. She had known. In a thousand ways. She picked up a brick from a stack beside the back door. Her husband ordered them five years ago, planned to lay a brick wall.

She hurled the brick at the house. It went through a window and amid all the crashing of glass she heard him say, "What the hell is this? Who did this?"

She didn't know. She didn't know a thing.

The Sister's Story

Reena wedged the box of silver carefully in the trunk of her Aunt Ovida's blue Olds, which was already full. Lord, Reena thought, what have I gotten myself into?

Aunt Ovida had packed boxes of food and dishes, plus her best lace tablecloth, a freshly pressed pink sheet and pink cloth napkins bought especially for the event.

"Why not use paper?" Reena asked.

Aunt Ovida snorted and for a moment didn't say anything, as if what Reena asked wasn't even worthy of an answer. Then she said, "You don't know women like that."

Women? Reena started to say, what women? Then it hit her. Women like *that*. Or to be specific *the* woman Uncle Lewis was seeing. Reena knew then what Aunt Ovida meant. But this whole things wasn't about his "restoration." That's what he was calling it these days, though Reena thought remodeling or reconstruction sounded better. Restoration usually meant, to her mind at least, something historical. The house wasn't historical, even if it had risen from the ashes.

Reena guessed to Uncle Louis it was a restoration all right. Two summers ago the whole house burned and everything in it. Only the brick shell, smoke stained, charred, roof dripping like melted plastic stood in the middle of a dozen dazed, burnt trees. Every fire truck in Wilson had been on the scene, every fireman.

They just stood and looked. Boom. Out of control. The whole thing was unbelievable. And Uncle Louis had done it.

"He has no one to blame but himself," Aunt Ovida said. "I wouldn't be a bit surprised if the insurance company refuses to pay a cent. It would serve him right."

Then a thought flickered through Ovida's mind and her expression changed.

The same thought hit Reena about the same time.

If Uncle Louis didn't have a house to livein, he might move in with Aunt Ovida and that wouldn't work for six minutes.

Aunt Ovida added, her voice softened a little and her eyes not quite so hard, "After all that's happened, he didn't deserve this too. Even if it is his own fault."

Reena knew Ovida meant the business about Aunt Charlotte. How Uncle Louis had killed her. Plain and simple. The evidence was there. He admitted on the six and eleven o'clock television news. In black and white in newspapers. "I couldn't help it," he said. "I couldn't stop. I hit the brakes, but the car wouldn't stop."

He meant the new car. The first new car they'd bought in twenty years. He drove wrecks. Not because he couldn't afford a new car, but because he was tight as a jar lid, Aunt Ovida said. He and Aunt Charlotte watched every penny like it was their first, last and only one. Uncle Louis couldn't repair or even attempt to work on the newer model cars. Ones with computers and fancy stuff. He didn't trust mechanics, didn't like to pay for something he could do himself, so he bought old cars and drove them until he couldn't get parts. Then he parked the hulking, sulking giant turtle shells of metal and wires in his garage. He had three wrecks parked there when the house burned. The fourth he drove. It caught fire when he shot WD40 on the car air conditioner that acted up. The gas tank exploded and the whole house went up like a rocket. That's what neighbors said and people across town who saw the smoke and flames.

So he killed his wife and he burned his house down and he didn't mean to do either. He wasn't charged with committing crimes. Just considered accident prone and unlucky.

The insurance companies *had* paid, and for two years Uncle Louis dogged the contractors, heating and air conditioning installers, roofers, plumbers, electricians, tile men, floor layers, appliance people and painters. After they got the roof on, he'd moved back in and lived among the mess, making more.

Now he had the whole thing finished.

Reena had been the one to suggest he have an open house. She'd done it to cheer him up. Uncle Louis had gotten so discouraged with his contractor and all the people working on the house and just life in general. And who wouldn't, she'd said to her husband, Gervase Hill.

"You're going to put on the dog," Gervase said, "and it's a dog that doesn't need to be put on."

"Yes, it does," Reena said. "It's the least we can do after all he's been through."

"Least, huh?" Gervase said. "You two don't fool me a minute. You're going over there to spy on Louis. I smell it and he will too."

Aunt Ovida picked up on the open house idea right away. She took the ball and ran with it. Took the bull by the horns, as Gervase liked to say.

Aunt Ovida wrote Uncle Louis her menu, color scheme, made lists and planned the whole thing. "I want this done right," she told Reena. Then she laughed and cried when Louis wrote her he'd been to five supermarkets and couldn't find pink sugar. Would white do?

Aunt Ovida had written him her recipe for pink punch and since everything else in it was pink, he'd thought the sugar had to be too. "I worry about him," Aunt Ovida said. "He's lost without Charlotte."

Reena was worried how the whole thing was going to turn out. Last night at midnight pressing napkins she wished she had never agreed to be a part of this tea or open house or whatever Uncle Louis wanted to call it. She and Aunt Ovida had knocked themselves out planning the thing and fixing food and polishing silver, and what if nobody came?

Uncle Louis was supposed to send out invitations. Or Reena *hoped* he sent out invitations. He could be so quirky at times, he might have decided not to send them and nobody would come and all this work and worry for nothing.

And tight? Lord, he "was so close to Mr. Lincoln they might be Siamese twins," Aunt Ovida said. He might decide stamps cost too much and not send invitations. Reena wished she'd called him to make sure. She'd feel better.

But here she was with Aunt Ovida tooling over to Wilson, car jam packed full of food and party fixings and probably thinking the same thing.

"You think she'll show up?" Reena asked. Aunt Ovida drove. She always drove, though Reena was a perfectly good driver. Aunt Ovida herself taught Reena, said those classes in high school didn't do what they were supposed to do and she'd been the one to teach her, even parallel parking.

"Wild horses couldn't keep a woman like her away," Aunt Ovida said. She gripped the steering wheel as if it might get loose. "She'll want to get a good look at us. See if we're the type who'll try to talk sense into somebody like Louis."

"I can't wait to see what she looks like," Reena said.

"I got my own picture," Aunt Ovida said, "and it's not pretty."

From the first time Louis wrote them about his "new friend" who worked at the dress shop and like to go out to eat, shop and dance, Aunt Ovida had been suspicious.

"That's how he met Charlotte," she said. "The self-same way."

She tapped the steering wheel with her middle finger.

"In a dress shop?" Reena said.

"Dance," Aunt Ovida said. "USO dance. Charlotte said she saw him across the room, thought he was the handsomest man there and decided she'd marry him."

"Didn't Uncle Louis have any say in the situation?"

"Didn't matter. He was caught dumb as a fish." Aunt Ovida adjusted her rear-view mirror. "Some people think highways are regular racetracks and drive that way." She checked her side mirrors, pulled out to pass.

Aunt Ovida was no slouch behind the wheel. She'd driven on freeways, expressways from Maine to Florida, New York to St. Louis. In her younger days, she and friends drove her new red Ford cross-country to San Francisco, just wanted to see the other edge of the ocean, she said.

When they parked the car in the driveway at Louis' and started to unload, there wasn't a soul in sight.

Aunt Ovida beep beeped her horn. "Where is that man?"

The backdoor was unlocked, so they loaded their arms with food and platters, punch bowls and napkins, and felt their way actually into the house. When he built the house, Uncle Louis didn't have a light put over the stairs. Don't need one, he told Aunt Charlotte, who said all those years she was going to fall and break her neck and it would be his fault.

"Take a flashlight," he said. "If it bothers you all that much."

"Who wants to carry around a flashlight all day?" she used to say. "You and your war with Carolina Power and Light. I want no part of it. Just a little light to see by."

"Leave the door at the top of the stairs open and you got all the light you need," Uncle Louis said.

As it turned out Aunt Charlotte never fell down those stairs, but her death was on Louis' hands anyway.

When he had his house rebuilt, he didn't have a light put over the stairs then either.

"Might have cost him a nickel or two," Aunt Ovida muttered, trudging up the stairs. Then she let out a choice string of expletives strong enough to blast open the door. They didn't. She kicked the door with her foot. "I don't care if I dent the damn thing," she said. "I've got both hands full. He knows we're coming and should have had the door open."

The door turned out to be locked. Aunt Ovida got tired of kicking it, sat on the top step and waited. "He's got to be in there. And sooner or later, he'll hear us and come."

Reena sat on the bottom step, boxes beside her. The smell of warming pimento cheese wafted up. She thought maybe Uncle Louis had forgotten they were even coming. What if he'd forgotten the open house completely? What if he was in there stretched out on the floor dead or something?

Before long the lock turned and Uncle Louis stood in the lighted doorway.

Aunt Ovida nearly fell back into Reena's face. "Whoops," she said, catching herself, one hand on the wall.

"I was in the shower and didn't hear you knock," he said, his hair damp, shirt stuck to his body. He smelled like soap and shaving cream and looked a little sleepy.

As they came into the hall, Reena glanced into Uncle Louis' bedroom to see if there were any signs the woman had moved in. Or was staying there. No nightgown on the floor, blouse thrown across the back of a chair. Nothing but Uncle Louis' bed piled high with ten quilts and the dangle of an electric blanket cord. Uncle Louis was extremely cold-natured and left the electric blanket on his bed year round. Nobody could sleep with him. Aunt Charlotte moved out twenty years ago. The bed he never made. "Waste of time," he said. "You just get right back in it." Any woman would have insisted on smoothing it at least.

Aunt Charlotte's room was on the left and both blinds were pulled tight. There were no signs anyone had been in it, or ever disturbed the dust three inches thick on the dresser.

Reena started to unpack some of the food, put it in the refrigerator when Aunt Ovida said, "Stop."

"What?" Reena looked around. Then she knew. Uncle Louis' kitchen looked like the first load here. Newspapers stacked chin high on every surface, bottles and jars, clean and washed, stood upside down on dishtowels beside the sink. On the stove nestled pots and pans five and six deep.

"Lord," Aunt Ovida said, "did you ever see such a sight? He didn't do one thing I told him."

"I got lemonade," Uncle Louis said from the stairs, where he'd carried up two boxes, his chin resting on the table linens. "Pink."

"I told you to get someone in to clean this house," she hissed. She had sucked in her breath until she loomed large with air and anger. "Nothing's been touched since the last time I was here."

Aunt Ovida had been to Wilson a dozen times since Aunt Charlotte's death, cleaned and shopped and left Uncle Louis written instructions on how to keep things organized.

"Nobody can live this way," she said, sweeping a stack of newspapers off the table with her arm. "These go to the garbage. They should have gone weeks ... months ago."

"Wait," Uncle Louis said. "I recycle."

"Well, you haven't lately." She swept up another stack and dumped them in the garbage can, which was surprisingly empty and freshly lined with a brown bag.

"The woman just left," Uncle Louis said.

"The woman! The woman!" Aunt Ovida almost screamed it out. "That woman?"

Reena knew what she meant. She waited for Uncle Louis to blush and own up or deny her.

"The cleaning woman," Uncle Louis said.

"Oh." Aunt Ovida almost dropped another stack of papers she'd lifted from the tabletop.

"You told me to get one," he said.

"Well, it didn't do you much good." Aunt Ovida sniffed, wiped the table clean with the blade of her hand. “I can’t see one thing she did … *if* she did anything.”

“She hadn’t had breakfast.” Uncle Louis lowered the boxes to the freshly bared table.

“What’s that got to do with the price of beans in China?” Aunt Ovida snapped.

“I couldn’t expect someone to work on an empty stomach, could I?” Uncle Louis said. “So I made her breakfast.”

“And you paid her, I guess,” Aunt Ovida said, gathering up bottles and jars, heading toward the trash. “Then took her home.”

“She said she’d come back.” Uncle Louis looked as if he wanted to snatch back his jars and run with them.

“I bet she will. I just bet she will.” Aunt Ovida disappeared down the stairs.

Reena checked the dining room. It was freshly vacuumed, the table polished. The whole room smelled like wax. The cleaning woman had done something. If not much.

Aunt Ovida swept into the room. “Where’s the leaf?” she called back to the kitchen. “You’re gonna need the leaf.”

“I think it was burned in the fire,” Uncle Louis called back.

Some of the furniture had been rescued, Reena remembered. Neighbors helped carry out a few things before the fire trucks got there. This table was one of the things saved.

“I had it refinished,” he said from the doorway. “And they lost the leaf.”

“That beats all,” Aunt Ovida said. “That just beats all. How am I supposed to fix a table that looks like anything when it's not big enough to ... to ... feed a cat on?" She looked ready to tune up and cry.

Reena felt like throwing up. The table was hardly bigger than a postage stamp and would never hold half the food they'd brought, much less a punch bowl. Then she spied the sideboard. "Let's put the punch on that." She pointed.

Aunt Ovida brightened a little. "We don't even have flowers and now there's no room."

Reena remembered how there were no flowers at Aunt Charlotte's memorial service and the ones on her grave ... where they buried the urn with her ashes in it ... had been bought by Aunt Ovida. "I couldn't bear the thought of that stark, empty red dirt staring back at us," she said. Aunt Ovida thought of things like that. She also thought of what people would say if there wasn't a single flower on Charlotte's grave. Someone in the community would notice and comment. As they would if word got back that Uncle Louis was dating "and that wife of his not cold in her grave." Was Aunt Ovida worried about what people would say or that the wrong kind of woman would move in and take advantage of Uncle Louis' loneliness?

"Spend everything he had and then some," Aunt Ovida said when she read Uncle Louis' letter. Uncle Louis wrote every week. That was one of the dear things about him. And he remembered everybody in the family at every occasion with a card. All the birthdays. And minor mishap or illness Aunt Ovida wrote him about or mentioned, he'd send a card. There was a sensitive nature to him. Maybe that's why Aunt Ovida worried someone would move in on him, marry him in a minute and strip him clean before he knew it.

They took stock of the rest of the house while Uncle Louis finished unloading the car.

"We won't even touch his bedroom," Aunt Ovida said. "I wouldn't know where to start." True you couldn't even see the floor for little hills and mountains of clothes. Yet a neat row of shoes showed under the bed. All lined up as though he'd strung a wire to even them. They closed the door.

"I wish it locked," Aunt Ovida said.

"Maybe no one will open it," Reena said.

"Oh, there'll be someone wanting to see in every corner," Aunt Ovida said. "Pry."

They left the door open to Aunt Charlotte's room. Opened the blind. It had been the least damaged by the fire. "There'll be some curiosity seekers. Wanting to see this room. Her room. As if that would tell them anything."

"It is an open house," Reena said.

"But that doesn't mean we have to open the whole house. They can just look at a few rooms and go home. If anybody shows up."

Almost before Aunt Ovida finished her sentence the doorbell rang.

"Lord!" She flew toward the kitchen. "You get that. I've got a million things to do. The nerve of somebody coming this early."

Somebody was only Ellen from next door with an arrangement of flowers.

"These were delivered to my house by mistake," she said. "I don't know why they do these things when Louis' name is right here on the envelope."

Who knows why anything? Reena thought. Anybody, anywhere, everybody, everywhere, everything. She opened the envelope, read the card, "My chance to do something for all you've done for me." It was signed, "Love, Dovie." Reena slid the card into her pocket. If Aunt Ovida saw that she'd explode into a tirade about "*that* woman!"

Reena put the flowers in the center of the table.

Aunt Ovida came from the kitchen with a tray of sandwiches in each hand. She put them down, moved the flowers over and smiled for the first time today. "I'm so glad Louis did one thing I wrote him to. And he didn't skimp like I was afraid he would."

Uncle Louis came up from the basement, banging as he came. "I almost forgot the veggies."

Veggies? Veggies was not an Uncle Louis word. He'd picked it up from somewhere or somebody.

Aunt Ovida looked at the deli arrangement and sniffed. "Louis, I told you I was bringing the food. We don't need that."

"There's another one down there," he said and inclined his head toward the hall, the basement door.

"Well, leave it. Take it back." Aunt Ovida waved her hand. "You spent money you didn't have to. Money you could have used on soap and water to clean this place up."

Reena took the tray of cut vegetables.

Aunt Ovida whirled toward the kitchen. "We don't have room for them and we ..."

"They're what Dovie said to get." Uncle Louis looked at his feet.

"I might have known," Aunt Ovida said. "You'd listen to anything *she* said when I wrote you plainly I would bring the food."

"They're fine," Reena said. "I'll get the other tray when we need it."

"Well, don't expect me to eat any of it," Aunt Ovida said. "Not the first mouthful. I'd choke."

Reena was afraid Aunt Ovida was going to choke now. She was so red in the face, her cheeks puffed. She put Dovie's veggies on the coffee table.

For the next two hours the place was bedlam with all Uncle Louis' friends from the college where he'd taught thirty years, neighbors, people Aunt Charlotte worked with at mental health, church friends and Reena could have sworn perfect strangers saw the crowd and came in for free food. She mixed punch and poured punch and put out more food until everything was down to crumbs and nibbles. Even the second vegetable tray lay bare and empty.

The neighbor who saw the smoke and called 911 introduced herself. She'd been walking her baby when she saw smoke and flames shooting from the roof. "I've never been so scared in my life."

She lived across the street in the subdivision Uncle Louis fought claw and beak when it was rezoned. "I've seen the place underwater," he said. "And I'll see it again. Only this time there'll be houses on it. It's not land to build on." A dozen houses had been built on the rise above the water meadow and a bridge across the flood plain.

Somewhere in the crowd, at some point, Reena noticed a woman wearing an orange pantsuit the color of Tang with hair dyed to match. She didn't look like any of Uncle Louis' or Aunt Charlotte's co-workers or neighbors or church people. The tunic top to her pantsuit was printed with a gold design. She wore a wide gold belt studded with various colors of plastic shapes, dangling gold things at her ears and on her wrists. And clear plastic shoes with gold colored heels. She didn't speak to anybody, and once when Reena was nearly out of punch, Aunt Ovida nowhere in sight, the woman in orange ducked into the kitchen and refilled the bowl.

"Thanks," Reena said.

"Don't mention it," the woman said and winked a thick blue eyelid at Reena. The blue was a peacock blue.

Dovie, Reena thought. Everything about her says so. "You must be Dovie."

"The one and only." The woman laughed. She patted her hair with both hands. Hands that had long, teal-colored nails. "I must look a mess," she said. "There's a fan blowing somewhere in this house." She looked toward the bedroom.

"I think he turned on the air conditioning," Reena said.

"Well." Dovie looked in the mirror above the sofa. The mirror and sofa Aunt Ovida chose and Uncle Louis bought out of his insurance money. "This *is* a momentous occasion when he turns on the AC."

Uncle Louis was the only person Reena ever heard call air-conditioning AC. He hated it. Said, "That stuff makes people sick if you ask me." Nobody did. Aunt Charlotte said it was paying the bill that sickened him. She was the one who air-conditioned the house after she retired. "I didn't know how nice it was until I tried to live without it." She turned it on; Uncle Louis wore sweaters and slept under quilts.

Dovie moved several chairs around, straightened the mirror, wiped dust off the top with those blue-green nails, motioned Reena to hand her a napkin. "I guess the woman did as much as she could in three hours. You can't expect miracles."

Reena wished Aunt Ovida would come back. She'd gone, laughing and talking, out the front door to see some of the people to their cars. People she'd met at Aunt Charlotte's memorial service and neighbors she'd gotten to know the times she'd been here with Uncle Louis. Where are you, Aunt Ovida? Reena said under breath as she leaned over the punch bowl. She drained the dregs, which was scarcely half a cup and drank it. She'd forgotten to eat lunch and also just realized how thirsty she was.

Dovie helped her carry things to the kitchen, ran water in the sink and began to wash them. From a drawer, she pulled out a dishcloth and drying towels and set to work.

"He's a good dancer," Dovie said, up to her elbows in soapsuds.

"Who?" Reena asked drying plates, cups, bowls and stacking them.

"Louie, Louie." She laughed. "That's what we call him."

She wore a perfume that smelled like wisteria. The same scent Aunt Charlotte used. Had Uncle Louis bought it for her or was it a coincidence? God, Reena thought, she'll get him now. If she wants him and Aunt Ovida swears that's what it's all about. Where was Aunt Ovida? Reena stood on tiptoes, peered out the window and picked out the back of Aunt Ovida's gray head in the dwindling group. She had pulled Ellen from next door over to one side and they looked to be in serious conversation, Aunt Ovida gesturing toward the house with one hand, Uncle Louis the other. He stood at the end of the driveway, talking to some of his bridge group, couldn't hear anything she said.

Reena and Dovie cleared the dining room table, folded the cloth and sheet. "She can wash these at home," Reena said.

"I'd offer to do them for her," Dovie said, "but she wouldn't trust me with her lace tablecloth."

There were several pink circles where people had set punch cups. Reena hoped they'd wash out. Aunt Ovida might leave the tablecloth to her someday, if she didn't get in a tizzy and toss it to Goodwill. She'd been known to do that. On a whim.

"I really appreciate your help," Reena said. "I never dreamed so many people would come. He must have invited half the town."

"I don't know a soul," Dovie said. She wiped crumbs from the table with the edge of her hand, emptied them in a vase on the mantel.

Reena packed boxes to carry home.

Dovie stood in the doorway. "I want you to know I'm not out to marry him."

Reena stopped. She hadn't asked.

"Oh, he wants me to and he offered me a diamond. Tried to give me hers and when I wouldn't take it, told me to go pick one out. But it's not that. I just want someone to go out with." She waved her hand in the air. "Marriage is for the birds. I ought to know. I've tried it five times."

Reena sucked in her breath. Five times. Lord, if Aunt Ovida heard that ...

"I'm not serious and he'll get over whatever notion he's got, or go on to somebody else." Dovie collected her purse from somewhere. A gold quilted evening bag on a long, loose chain. She headed toward the front door. "Bye, now." She waved a five-fingers wave, a little blur of blue-green, like a hummingbird.

Reena looked for Aunt Ovida. Nowhere. Uncle Louis, at the end of the driveway, talked to Ellen, the last to leave. But where was Aunt Ovida?

Then Reena saw her. Bent over, head in the car trunk, packing boxes. Turn around and look, Reena said under her breath. She tapped on the window. Aunt Ovida didn't hear her. She tapped louder.

Dovie walked down the front walk, turned and waved again to Reena in the window. Then she hugged Uncle Louis, kissed him on the cheek and left. He reached after her, missed, stood there with his arm in midair.

On the way home, Aunt Ovida said, "I knew she wouldn't show up."

"Who?" Reena was more tired than she thought. She knew who, but she didn't know what to say.

"Didn't have the decency to show her face. Sneak around and hide. Her kind always do."

"She was there," Reena said.

"What?" Aunt Ovida hit her brakes to keep from going into the car in front that suddenly slowed. "I certainly didn't see her if she was there."

"I did," Reena said. "She seemed nice."

"Nice!" Aunt Ovida almost screamed the word. "Nice!"

"Nice to me," Reena said. "She helped me clean and pack up."

"Why didn't you call me?" Aunt Ovida said.

Reena didn't know if she meant to help and pack up or to meet Dovie.

"Where was I?" Aunt Ovida sounded angry. "I was there the whole time and I didn't see anybody that could even remotely be her. And I would have known if I'd seen her."

"You were there. She walked right by you."

Aunt Ovida snorted. It was plain she didn't believe Reena. "I knew she wouldn't come. I knew it the whole time. But I'll meet her yet. I just hope before it's too late."

"It's not too late," Reena said.

"I hate getting home this late," Aunt Ovida said. "And tired to boot. I won't sleep a wink tonight. Not one wink."

The Preacher's Story

The Kitchen Sink

When Tobin Ellis opened the front door he saw dust where their furniture had been. A crack in the wall ran ceiling to floor where the china cabinet stood. Light from the opened drapes shone a dusty path across the bare floor.

"Joyce," he called. The word echoed.

She even took the parsonage rugs. Damn.

His footsteps sounded large and his legs felt hollow as he checked the kitchen. There were indentations on the red linoleum where the chairs had been, four pockmarks the size of saucers from the table legs. The kitchen table he'd bought at an auction, scraped the finish off and painted five coats of white until it gleamed like milk. He felt the empty air. Every cabinet door hung open and every shelf stood stark and bare, except under the sink, far in a back corner, he found a can of cleanser. He shook it into the sink and scoured with a paper towel. He made circles, then circles onto those circles. In the empty house the sound of his scrubbing echoed and the echoes chased around in his head. "She won't be back. She won't be back."

When he heard someone call, he stopped, turned toward the living room, can of cleanser clutched to his chest.

"Pastor Ellis?"

For a moment, only one, his heart caught. Maybe. But he knew it wasn't Joyce.

Drema Turner from across the street stood in the doorway, the hard orange afternoon light carved her thick silhouette like a life-sized cardboard character. She bent forward, poised for whatever calamity that waited. She was ready. "Everything all right?"

She knew damn good and well it wasn't. He wanted to shout, but he chewed the inside of his cheek, took a little breath and waited. She knew more about all this than he did, but he didn't want to hear it. Not now. He slid to the floor in front of the sink, held the cleanser. The woman on the label looked like Drema. She held a hatchet and chased a chicken. He felt like that chicken.

"I'm fixing to put Thurman's supper over and I've got extra. I'll set a plate for you."

He couldn't see her face, but her voice sounded softer than usual, every word wrapped in a thin, sad dampness.

"No," he said, "I'm not hungry."

"You come all that way and ..."

"And what?" He held the cleanser up. "And you know my sweet little wife didn't have supper or anything else hot waiting for me." He hoped she'd see the shine of the can and think it was beer. That would send her back out the door faster than she came in and straight to the telephone. She'd get the gossip line going and before ten o'clock tonight every member of his church would know that not only had the preacher's wife up and left, but there he was sitting on the kitchen floor drinking like a fish. He started to laugh.

The story would have him drunk, surrounded by a dozen beer cans and talking about suicide. They would say he was pacing and cursing, out of his head with grief and worry and no wonder she left ... if he was an alcoholic. Of course, they'd say, nobody could ever see what he saw in her in the first place. She was such a stuck-up little thing. Never spoke more than two words to anybody in that whole church. Said a minister's wife was entitled to her own life. The church didn't hire her. She had a job. Fine job at that. Dressing to the teeth and prancing around that law office all day. Nobody could get any work done in five-inch heels. All you had to do was look at those nails to know she never did much more than pick up a piece of paper or two. She never typed. Not with those hands.

Tobin knew they said she certainly didn't do anything around the house. That the kitchen door was kept closed but once Drema had darted in before Joyce could stop her and what she'd seen had been enough to make her halt in her tracks. The sink was stacked ... yes, stacked ... with what looked like a month's worth of dirty dishes. "Why, I don't even own that many dishes," Drema said.

Now, today, she said, "I just thought I'd help out."

"I think you're too late," he said. He sprinkled cleanser on the floor, scrubbed at a soiled spot near his shoe. The stain looked like spaghetti sauce. When had they had spaghetti? He couldn't remember. He couldn't remember the last meal they ate together in this house.

Playing around. Of course, he knew she was playing around. There wasn't anything he could do about it. Oh, he'd tried to let Joyce know he knew. Funny thing was, she didn't try to hide it. The red roses in the bedroom. When she saw him look at them, she said she'd sent them to herself. "I have to. You're so deep in those dusty old books in that library, you don't know there are people alive and walking on this earth, much less hungry."

"Hungry?" he'd asked. "The church feeds the hungry."

"You don't know the hungry I'm talking about."

He knew she was taken care of. And would be even better when he finished seminary. He only had eighteen more months of commuting. He couldn't help it this church was three hours from school. It was a place to start and this little church in the backwoods she laughed at was paying his way. And hers. She spent everything she made on her back. He knew expensive clothes and shoes and jewelry and underwear when he saw them. Silk. Handmade. She said she ordered those panties from somewhere. Said anything else close to her skin irritated.

He hadn't said anything.

"It's not good to go on grieving over spilt milk," Drema Turner said.

He had forgotten Drema was there.

She reached up and gathered a cobweb from across the doorway, walked toward the sink to wash her hands. When she reached for a paper towel she turned around and waved her hands in the air, drying them. "No use wanting what ain't there," she said with a little laugh.

That was how he felt.

"They can build overnight," she said.

"What?" He looked at her feet, large feet that seemed spread almost flat in a wide, brown sandal. He knew he should stand up, but he couldn't. His legs didn't feel as if they were attached to the rest of him.

"Spider webs," she said. "They can build overnight. Why, one morning I got up and there was one clear across my kitchen sink and no spider in sight."

"She's gone," he said.

"I shouldn't say it, but I will." Drema looked out the kitchen window. "Good riddance to bad rubbish."

That was when he grabbed those bony legs above those flat brown sandals and pulled them to the floor.

Drema shrieked like a drowning cat. "What? Don't ... don't ... don't!" She slapped at him, tried to push his hands away, uncurl his fingers from her ankles. She kicked him and the kicks bounced off.

"Preacher," she spluttered when she got loose. She lay on her back like a beached whale and spouted up air. "Preacher, be ashamed of yourself."

He stood then, picked up the can of cleanser and sprinkled it all over her.

She waved her arms, covered her face, coughed and gagged. "I never," she said. "I never did ... all I was trying to do was be a good neighbor. Do my duty as a Christian."

When the can was empty, he dropped it on her stomach and stepped back.

She cried now, great blue tears that rolled down her cheeks to the floor and puddled.

He'd never seen tears puddle before.

"There are people who will hear about this," she said, sucking in her breath as she got to her feet. She brushed the cleansing powder off herself, patted and shook and stamped her feet. The powder was green and white and smelled like mothballs. "You don't go around treating people this way and get off without paying a price."

"I paid!" he shouted. "I paid with everything I got and then some."

She went out the front door, left it open.

Tobin went out the back door to the clothesline, unpinned the single pair of white silk panties from it, folded them carefully and slid them in his shirt pocket. They fit right behind the notebook paper where he'd written Sunday's sermon. Neither were any good now.

He left the clothespins on the line. They held up nothing.

The Single Woman's Story

She hadn't even washed the biscuit flour off her hands that morning when the knocking began. Knocking on that old door so strong she thought the glass would loosen. The glass stayed firm—it was everything else that let go. Let go and let him in. Him in that dark blue suit and red-striped tie. Him that looked for all the world like that somebody she'd waited for all her life. And the feeling that came over her. Warm and electric. Like lightning starting at her scalp, zinging down her face and neck, lifting up her breasts, pulling in her waist and not stopping there. No, going in and tugging her inside till she had to cross her legs and hold onto the door to keep from falling over.

"Miss Broom?" he said. "I'm Densmore Toole from the Evermore Insurance Company." He smiled those pearly whites and she was blinded by the light behind him, in and through him, coming straight off his face. It was like Moses and the burning bush and she wanted to say, "Yes, Lord, tell me what you want."

"May I come in?" he asked and slid his briefcase in first. A fine leather briefcase ... burgundy, sleek, and soft. She reached for the briefcase. He took her hand instead, shook it, and she didn't want him to ever let go. His hand so small and warm and she wanted to put it between her breasts, press the rest of him there too. He indicated the sofa. "Is it okay if I sit here while we talk?"

She felt herself nodding. He could sit anywhere he wanted. He could sit in her lap. She giggled.

Miss Lettie started to move the stack of magazines and newspapers and he stopped her. "It's okay," he said and laid his briefcase across his knees.

She stood behind the rocking chair, holding the posts, and rocking the thing back and forth like her heart felt, pendulum on a clock swinging so good and steady, saying yes, yes, yes. Then the first smell of burning biscuits made her trot as fast as she could down that long, cold hall toward the kitchen.

Lo and behold, she turned around after taking the burnt biscuits out and there he stood, his smile the sweetest thing, half-laughing and half-sorry. "My fault, I'm afraid," he said. "I interrupted your work."

"No, no," she finally said something. "This oven's never been one you could trust." She dumped the biscuits into the trash, where they rolled off the baking sheet like wooden wheels loosened from a broken toy. "I've got more." She lifted little white moons of dough and laid them ever so carefully one by one in the pan, shoulders touching. He watched wide-eyed as a child.

"Church," she said.

"Not communion?"

"No, no... these are for the ham supper. Our fundraising." When they asked her to do them again this year, she said, "They'll be my last." Nobody seemed to have heard her. Lucritia

Motts just wrote down her name and twelve dozen beside it. "I'll be baking biscuits when Gabriel blows his horn, I guess." She laughed for the first time in weeks.

He saw the coffee pot, took a cup from the shelf and poured it full. "Black as sin," he said. "Anything else isn't coffee."

She put the biscuits in. He'd refilled her own cup.

"That's the way I like it too," she said. "Black and strong enough to walk out of here." He seemed natural as air sitting across from her. "You live alone?" He looked around the kitchen, taking in her geraniums blooming pale and hungry against the glass. She didn't know why she bothered year after year to haul plants in; they filled the room so. That and Mama's old wood stove. Nothing cooked like that stove when the weather was right and you had your mind on what you were doing. She saw him taking in the stacked counters of jars. "You put up a lot of vegetables?"

"All I can," she said and twisted her tumbling-down hair back into the knot atop her head. She bet she looked a mess and here he was so clean, even his forehead shined. His hair looked dark as the dark under the quilts on her bed. She'd always slept with her head under the covers and all her life everybody said she'd smother herself to death. Well, she hadn't. And they'd all died before her. Ha. And Frances Elizabeth, who used to be after her all the time about sleeping under so much cover, went and died first. Lettie bet that just galled her to death.

"Ha," he said. "All you can." When he laughed Lettie saw silver fillings in his teeth way back. She'd had false teeth so long, she forgot about things like fillings. False teeth you just put them in and went and forgot they were on until you went to bite something. Of course, it never stopped her much from eating what she wanted. Maybe he was hinting he wanted one of her biscuits. She got up and opened the oven door to check them, letting that hot, brown smell fill the room.

"My mama had a stove like that," he said. "She baked the best biscuits ever touched my lips. I always said I'd marry any woman who could cook like my mama."

"You did?" Inside her heart caught, revved up to whirl.

"Then I went and didn't. Let my head outrun my stomach and I been sorry ever since."

"You're married?" Miss Lettie almost dropped the jar of fig preserves she'd gotten up to open.

"More married than I want to be," he said and closed his eyes. "Married to a woman who'd shoot me in my sleep if I so much as looked at somebody else. Oh, I've had chances heaped upon chances." He put more sugar in his coffee and stirred. "In my line of work ... why, I'm in and out of a dozen homes a day and no neighbor thinks a thing about it. My reasons are sweet as a preacher's. There's some I could take advantage ... bereaved and wanting or wanting what they never had." He took the fig preserves she handed him and a spoon and began to eat out of the jar. He didn't look at her.

He didn't say thank-you-fine-preserves-Miss-Lettie-you're-a-good-cook-Miss-Lettie-I-appreciate-you-letting-me-come-in-that-was-good-coffee-Miss-Lettie. Nothing. He ate like she'd canned the whole jar for him and nobody else. She liked a little preserves on her biscuits too, and here he was helping himself.

She smelled the biscuits brown and getting browner. She didn't get up to check them and when the smoke started curling at them, she just kept pretending to read the policy paper he'd pulled out. The smell got darker and darker and it was all she could do not to jump up, yank them out and start fanning the smoke with a dishtowel.

"Lord God," he finally said, "you're burning your biscuits."

Your biscuits, she started to say, but smiled and smiled. "Maybe," she said. "Maybe."

He leaped from the chair, grabbed at the pan of biscuits, dropped them and hopped back, dancing, the biscuits raining around him like her hopes, falling and rolling around his feet and toward the door like they expected him to follow.

The New Woman's Story

She sat on the edge of the bed.

He paced.

She looked out the window. Below them, the ocean raged. She thought, I wish I could walk through those windows onto the beach, into the water and keep walking. She wished she could walk to the other side of the ocean.

"You did it on purpose," he said.

"What?" She looked at the floor. Beige carpet. New. The color of sand. That's practical, she thought, even for an expensive hotel.

"You know perfectly well *what.*" He stood in front of her, his belt buckle level with her eyes. She had that buckle made with his initials, RWB. She thought he'd be pleased. Instead, when he opened the package, he peeled back the paper and lifted out the buckle without a comment. Later she asked him if he liked it. "I'm wearing it, aren't I?" And mumbled something about it being heavy and if he'd wanted such a thing, he would have bought it for himself. That's all he ever said.

"I don't have any idea what you're talking about," she said. And she didn't. Not really. Plus, she was too tired to care. She felt as if she had sharp seeds of sand behind her eyelids. Itchy, stinging burr-like seeds. He held the TV clicker up like a prize. Something he had and she wanted. She didn't. Behind them a black and white Western played, grainy and sad. A man galloped a horse across the screen. The horse hoofs sounded heavy and hollow as if they hit wooden boards.

"You have done this too many times lately for me to think it was anything but done deliberately." He slapped the palm of his hand with the clicker.

She truly couldn't think why he was mad at her. She couldn't think of a thing she had done to anger him. No big sins. Not even a small sin. Though sometimes it took only parking her car too near the center of the driveway to set him off. Then he had to park two wheels on the grass so he could open his door. Just another one of her thoughtless, self-centered acts, he said. She hadn't noticed. She'd had an armload of groceries, a briefcase full of work and her purse. "So paint a line where you want me to park," she said, but he didn't. Besides, there was a grassless rut beside the drive where she parked when *he* got home first. The drive was not big enough for two cars.

Neither was the house. In the den he threw newspapers around, watched sports, clicking from soccer to wrestling to professional basketball all at once. She had reports to read, spreadsheets to study, statements to prepare. He said they didn't pay her enough to bring work home. He said if she was efficient, like *he* was, she'd get everything done before five or walk away and leave it. You won't get any gold stars for killing yourself, he said. She said it wasn't that. These were a couple of accounts she'd volunteered to do. Several small businesses that were individually owned and needed closer attention than others.

"Women's lib stuff," he'd said. "I hope you get your fill of that." Then added, "Don't come crying to me when nobody notices. Nobody pats you on the head."

Last year she had gotten a plaque at the women's commission banquet.

"Try taking that to the mall," he said. "See how far it goes."

It had taken her to this conference, all expenses paid (and his too, but she'd bite her tongue before she reminded him), where she'd given a talk on "First Year Financial Management for the Small Businesswoman." Her talk had gone over well, with loud applause and good response during the question and answer session. Several people mentioned they'd like her to come to St. Louis or Boston and present it there. And the honoria mentioned were larger than the one here. Things looked good. She was excited. And happy. Until the banquet.

He hardly spoke during the meal, except to complain his roast beef was overcooked. He liked it rare. Had asked for it rare. Which made her shudder, seeing the red flesh float in blood juices on his plate.

"Send it back," she said.

"They won't get it any better the next time," he said, chewing hard, his jaw like a vise. People still congratulated her at the banquet on her speech. She introduced him to the ones she knew. Friends who turned to him and said things like they bet he was proud of her and so on. He managed a tight smile, nodded and continued to butter his roll, cut his meat or drown his salad with dressing.

Afterwards they went to the bar for a nightcap.

He said he had a headache. She asked if he wanted aspirin. There was some in her purse. He said he didn't need aspirin, clenched his teeth and turned away. She suggested he go back to their room and she'd come later.

He said, "No, if I do that, you'll stay here until midnight. If I'm here," he emphasized the last word, "at least you'll be reminded I exist."

She turned to say that remark was not becoming and he certainly didn't need to make himself miserable on her behalf, but about that time someone leaned over her shoulder and asked her to join their table.

"Go on," he said, flicking the back of his hand. "I'll stay at the bar. The godawful band's not so loud here."

"I won't be long," she said. And she wasn't. Several times she motioned him to join them and he shook his head. After a while she noticed he wasn't there, so she excused herself and went to their room. Maybe he was feeling worse than a headache.

He stood, back to the door, stared out the window. They were on the fifteenth floor, but from the balcony their room looked level with the sea.

"Get some fresh air." She slid open the doors. "You'll feel better."

He didn't move. Instead he clicked on the TV, turned to watch it. A game show played in bright reds, blues, yellows, with a wheel that spun slowly flashing numbers. "Sixteen, twenty-seven, thirty-three."

She thought, that's my life. I've gone round in a circle and the numbers still don't make sense. Nothing balanced. She sat on the bed, took off her shoes, rubbed her feet back and forth on the nubby carpet.

He paced between the queen size beds.

She noticed how wide his belt was. Brown leather. She remembered her father always wore a wide belt. He used to threaten with it. "If you kids don't stop that, I'll take my belt to you." He never hit her with it. He never hit her at all. But her brothers got whipped with that belt for many things, many times. She remembered their terror, the sound of her father's belt as it whistled through the air, the whack, the cracking whack of it as the belt hit their bare backs. She never watched, but from the other bedroom heard their cries. And afterwards saw the red streaks across their shoulders, welts the belt made. "Miss Goody Goody," her brothers called her. "Little Miss Perfect. Miss Priss." She wasn't perfect and she learned how to lie.

"Think you know it all," her husband said now.

"I don't know what you mean," she said. His voice had the same sound as her brothers' when they called her "Miss Perfect. Daddy's Pet."

"Sure you do," he said and flicked the channel.

"Red wolves are being reintroduced into their natural habitat," the nature announcer said. On the TV there was a mother wolf and four pups. "The female wolf weans the pups at twenty-four months of age, leaving them to fend for themselves in the wild."

"You talked to everybody in that bar but me," he shouted.

Maybe she had. She didn't think about it. She knew a lot of people there. "So what stopped you?"

"I didn't know anybody there," he said. His voice had a whine to it, like a six-year old.

"You could get to know somebody." She picked at the coverlet, traced the pattern of ivy with her finger until it twined with red and pink poppies. She'd never noticed before how much poppies looked like anemones. She'd planted anemones once. The first winter they were married, after the miscarriage. She bought the ugly little bulbs when they barely had enough money to buy food. He never noticed. He liked the tuna casseroles. Once, when the anemones bloomed in the snow, she went out barefoot in her nightgown at midnight, bent over and buried her face in them. They smelled like spring, a cold, clean spiciness with a hint of sweet. She could have eaten them, black petal by black petal, in the moonlight. During the day they were red and purple, blue and pink. He never noticed the flowers. If he had, she would have said they must have been planted by the people who lived there first.

"There wasn't anybody I wanted to know," he said.

Red wolves sat behind boulders and howled.

"How do you know? How could you tell?"

"Oh, I could tell all right. All those tight-ass fellows with their cute little walks and the waving of hands. A couple of bitches in black dresses cut down to their navels."

"Did you think they were trying to pick you up? Which sex?" The idea made her laugh. She laughed and laughed. She fell back on the bed laughing. God, she wished they had. That someone had picked him up, taken him out, taken him anywhere so she didn't have to go through this shit.

"You think you are so damn smart." He picked up one of her shoes, held it over her, heel close as a weapon. "I could smash your face in."

Laughter choked in her throat. She'd seen him angry, but she'd never seen him like this. There was nobody she knew in his eyes. Nobody. She felt cool air as he waved the shoe back and forth, the sharp heel inches from her face. Inches. The sole of her shoe was a tan blur. He stopped, held the shoe so close to her nose she caught the faint scent of leather, the rubber tip on the heel.

She didn't move.

Wolves on TV growled. She didn't look. Instead she watched his wrist and she saw something. She saw his wrist tremble. One small tremble. Then she knew. She knew he knew she would leave. She was as good as gone.

She reached for her shoe and he gave it to her, looked away. Looked at the TV. She slipped on her shoe. Found its mate and put it on too. Then she picked up her purse and walked to the door.

She didn't look back.

If she had, she would have seen him sitting on the bed changing channels, clicking, clicking, clicking.

The Lady Wrestler's Story

Dixie Vanilla's Gold

That Friday the trunk on my Cadillac popped open of its own accord. I thought, Cherry, you fool, somebody is trying to tell you something. And by durn if they weren't. Nothing I wanted to know, but you can only keep me in the dark so long, then the new day dawns and me with it. Ha!

You ever seen an honest-to-God gold Cadillac? I don't mean plated, nothing like that. Who could afford it? But gold colored and shiny as the sun when it's clean and polished. These gold jobs don't come easy, and mine was a hard-bruising time in the getting. I got x-rays of my bones to show for it. Which is more than Clifford T. can say for his. But that's not to say he won't from now on. Which is not something he was counting on. I, however, think it goes with the territory.

Anyway, there I was idling down Main Street, minding my own beeswax, me and Sugar (I named her after Elizabeth Taylor's dog), in her little doggie car seat, which everybody says is the cutest thing, when wham, the trunk lid sprung up again like somebody popped it. Bong! I thought, that's crazy or some joke. I knew there was nothing I had done and no way Sugar could have caused it, even if she wanted to, which I was sure she did not. So I hauled into the empty K-Mart parking lot that is all broken pavement, glass and weeds high as your waist, got out and looked to see if I could see anything different. I didn't. So I shut it and that's when the thought hit me again. Real hard this time. The thought, not the trunk lid. Clifford T. Richardson was cheating his balls on me. Banging somebody like there is no tomorrow, which in his case, I was about to make sure there wouldn't be. Clifford The Bastard. A sixty-year-old wheezing, hacking, hard-blowing stallion was about to be put out to stud pasture. Into the back barn. On the block. Up for bids. Dog meat. Ha!

I knew where to look. Where they all go to do it in the daylight hours. That old Howard Johnsons out on #54, the one with the witchy roof and little fat Hojo faded by the parking lot. I could have laughed out loud. Of course it would have scared the pee out of Sugar. The state I was in, and, if I'd started laughing, I'd have had a hell of a time stopping.

Did Clifford T. think I didn't have the sense God gave a gobble turkey? That I wouldn't come check?

Sure enough, there he was parked out front. GLOW sticker on his back bumper just like mine. Glorious Ladies of Wrestling. His Cadillac is big and black as a hearse, which is what I meant was going to carry them away while Sugar and I watched.

I was wearing nothing but my new fur coat, fake of course, but looking real enough to fool most people, and pink satin mules. The kind with pom poms and clear plastic heels. I just love those things, and I didn't intend to get them dirty. If I'd had on decent shoes I might have gotten out, gone in and said a few things I'd want to take back later, but as it turned out, I let my foot do the talking. It stomped that gas pedal and wouldn't let up. Wham, bam, over the curb and up the walk, through the door and here I come. There he was in those big red boxer shorts I gave him last Valentine's. Shorts with little silver hearts all over them and a lock and key printed on the front opening which I thought was cute then, not so cute now. Depends on where you wear them and with whom. With *whom* was he going to take up next? Ha!

It might be a good long while before he gets his pecker in working order, not to mention presentable to members of the opposite sex. The opposite sex of which I am proud to be an upstanding member.

Clifford T's mouth and that hussy's mouth hung open like pockets. His and Hers. As I drove through, she grabbed a blanket, wrapped herself in it, while he reached for the drapes and swaddled himself.

The whole thing was slow motion. Of course I wasn't going all that fast. Just straight and slow and steady.

When I went through the back wall, which was as flimsy as cardboard, and hit the Dempsey Dumpster, it sounded like all hell tore loose, but I just shoved the Caddy in reverse, whirled around and drove through the whole thing again. This time electric wires popped like firecrackers and light fixtures let loose, landed on my roof. Glass broke all around and shot out in all directions, not to mention that big mirror that went all silver sparks. Lord, it was like being in a Broadway show, which is something I always thought I'd like to try. Wear some sequined thing and ostrich feathers on my head and out my kazoo.

The metal doorframe bent and swung loose, the door on one hinge going whap, whap. The front and back walls fell down flat the first time I hit them. I've said for a long time these crackerjack motels were built like chicken crates. Now I was thinking it sure was a good thing. Otherwise I'd have been sitting outside that room with my front end nosing the door, tires spinning and motor gunned to go nowhere.

And the bed? That king-size job turned around and went through the wall to the room next door. She was hovering in that bed screaming her head off. I heard her over the radio and all the crashing going on too. She screamed like one long flashing blue siren. I knew she wasn't hurt and neither was he, but I hoped I scared the shit out of him. Or at least locked up his bowels into the middle of next week.

By this time, people started to gather in the parking lot. The manager ran out. He wore a turban and long skirt. Indian, I think. All the motels these days are owned by people from India and they're all named Patel. He shouted something. The rest of the crowd just looked on, waved their arms, smiled. I swear it was like half of them cheered me on, cleaning women with their carts and a couple of men from the service station across the road.

Sugar bounced up and down in her little seat and barked, so I couldn't hear a thing. Whatever they said, I didn't plan to stop.

I screeched that big gold baby around like the devil himself hollered my name and I aimed it toward that room again. This car was good as a tank. So far not even a window had cracked. Oh, I was going great. If the whole end of that motel went down this time, and those two got buried in the rubble, I didn't care.

When they got dug out, the newspaper could report what position they'd been found in and who with. I'd be somewhere else. Somewhere warm with palm trees and coconuts, laughing my tail off.

But I didn't get that far. Six police cars hauled in around and behind me. Those guys got out with guns and aimed the things smack at me. Had those big barrels right up to the window. Two policemen jumped on my hood, so I couldn't see a thing but blue uniforms and mad faces.

The police pulled at my door handles, put their feet up and tried to pry my doors open. Everything held, I am proud to say. Me and my Cadillac stayed tight. Like I said, it's built right. Built better than that motel. Maybe Cadillac could use me in their advertising. Show pictures of my car, me and the mess we made in only a few minutes of casual motoring. I wondered if I could say the car went out of control and there wasn't a thing I could do. Somehow I didn't think that would work.

"Open up or we'll pry you out of this can," one of the policemen shouted. He pounded on my driver's door.

I ran the window down a few inches, said, "Move on back now." I dangled the car keys, which they all started to reach for. "Not until you step back."

They stepped back but had me surrounded. I'd never seen so much blue. So much metal. All sides.

Then the manager pushed through and said some stuff I couldn't understand, rammed his fist toward my face, twisted it. "Sue, sue," he said. "My legal representative will sue. You will build me a bigger motel. A new motel. Sue. Sue you," he kept saying.

I unlocked the door, gathered Sugar in my arms and stepped out, one good-looking leg at a time, slowly. There have been people over the years who told me I was in the wrong end of show business. That I had dancer's legs. It's because I keep in shape. I've worked hard all my life. In my business you have to stay hard. And tough.

"Driver's license?" the closest police said. He'd put his gun away. So had the others who stood looking at the hole in the wall, what was left of the furniture, not to mention Clifford T. and that hussy too, standing in the middle of the room rubble now wrapped up like Arabs in blankets, just their little pink faces peeking through the folds.

I gave the policeman Sugar to hold and reached for my handbag. There was enough loose money in there; I thought about sliding some of it toward the policeman when I took Sugar, saying, "Let's forget this whole thing. My insurance company will fix the motel. No questions asked." I've bribed enough officials in my life. I know when and how, but something in this guy's eyes told me that this was not the time nor place. So I kept quiet, pulled my coat tight and let Sugar lick my face.

"Dixie Vanilla," he said, handed back my license. "I've seen you in the ring. I saw you take Wanda Steele in Charlotte Coliseum once. Wasn't that the world championship?"

"One of them," I said.

"I thought you died," he said. He couldn't have been more than thirty. Must have been a kid when he saw me take Wanda Steele.

"Not hardly," I said. "Just retired."

"Nah," he said, "You're not that old. You're in too good a shape." He patted my car fender. "Of course not as good a shape as this baby. I saw your picture in the paper when you won it." I thought again about the money in my purse. The other policemen poked through the ruins with the manager. They had their backs to us. One of them listened to Clifford T. while he pointed at me, then the motel mess. Clifford was barefooted and I bet his feet were cold as hell. They always were. I bet he'd catch the flu and be sick as a dog for a week and want me to bring him soup and rub his chest with goose grease. Goose grease! Whoever heard of such a thing? The last time he was sick, I got a can of lard and since he couldn't smell, he didn't know the difference. And he got well anyway. Of course he was saying things now like I tried to kill them and didn't a car count as a weapon? And she? Miss Hussy of 1997 had her head on the chest of the youngest policeman, crying all over him. He looked trapped and bored. I wondered if that was how Clifford T. felt with me. But marriage had not been my idea. Or maybe it had. I couldn't remember who mentioned it first.

All I knew was we'd won the big pot. We'd done the Garden and Ava Oscolot, the cat, had been a tub of butter beneath me all six rounds. And the crowd had been wild. Beer and confetti. Beer and confetti. That's what I remember. Balloons. Must have been a million. Then the next day there was the parade and a couple more parties. After all the hoopla petered out, I came home to start the school. Take me some young girls who had the build and weren't afraid to break bones, theirs included or maybe most of all. But the most important thing they had to have was want. They had to want the title and the belt so bad they'd work their tails off to get it.

Then I got soft. Clifford T. would say, you sleep late and I'll do the morning workouts. And the afternoons. I went shopping. Learned make-up, how to grow roses. Roses! The more he did, the less I worried about. Of course I still interviewed the girls. Country girls built like harvesting machines. Girls who grew up hard and hungry. I had nothing to worry about until one day I looked at the books. None of the figures made sense, so I went to the bank. There had to be some mistake. There was, and it was mine for ever trusting Clifford.

So I went home, shucked off every stitch I wore and went to bed naked as the day I came into the world, burning mad and shaking with shock. Until I heard the trunk lid on my Caddy pop up the first time. Sprong! And nobody there. Looked out my window. There it sat, open like my mouth when a lot of things began to add up. Afternoons he hadn't been at the gym when I called. Bank withdrawal slips and he never had any money. None. Clothes he took to the cleaners himself. He never did that before. How he was freshly showered when he came home and not wearing the same clothes as when he left. He said he liked to keep a change at the gym in case he got in the ring without putting on his warmup suit. Ha!

So where was he? Then I remembered the old Howard Johnsons we used to go to, got up, threw on the first thing my hand hit when I reached in the closet, which turned out to be my new fake fur coat that looks real as mink. Shoved my feet into the nearest shoes, which happened to be the pink satin mules, grabbed up Sugar, slammed out and into the car, driving like hell until I found them.

"Miss Vanilla," Sargent Roy Bivens, said, "I've radioed in and there's going to be some charges and things, but for right now, let's take you to the hospital to get checked out. I can't believe you'd come through all this without some shock."

"Oh, it's a shock, believe me," I said and got back in the car. "But I can drive my own self where I need to go." Which wasn't the hospital, but I didn't tell him.

"Department people will write all this up and call you in. We know you'll work with us."

I had tucked the money into the pad on his clipboard when I handed it back, and while I knew I'd be charged with a bunch of junk, none of it was anything I couldn't handle.

So I just put the dog in her little car seat and headed out, Cadillac purring like a battle-scarred lion, not even limping, air still in all four tires.

At the first traffic light I noticed something caught and flapping on the side mirror. I reached out and couldn't believe it when my fingers found them. I pulled those suckers in. Black. Lace. Panties. Not my size. I hung them from the rear mirror and drove on home, me and the dog laughing like fools.

The Clerk's Story

He only worked there, but he parked in front of the shop, angling in his little blue Datsun truck with the three bald tires and odometer reading a hundred fifty-six thousand miles.

Miss LidaSue's car was a black bus of a car; a black hearse of a car; a sperm whale of a Buick. She docked it in the back corner of the gravel lot at 9:01 every morning, where it belched and farted for a full five minutes after she took her foot off the gas.

Ed never knew her to be ten minutes late to work, though sometimes she did slam her car door as the last chime of the final hymn broadcast from the First Baptist Church.

She opened the lock with a key hung from a hook on her belt and swung open the back door so heavy Ed could have sworn it was studded with steel.

"Good morning," Miss LidaSue said as she walked past and up the stairs to her office. She never waited for him to answer and if he had anything to tell her, he either waited until she came down again or picked up the phone and dialed their own number. She picked up and said, "All right," like she was Mrs. God and he was reporting in. Then he said what he had to say. Except today. By damn if he was going to do it today.

Ed didn't know when he'd tell her, nor how. He just knew he had to do it today. Before

She stood on the platform above him, her she found out. Before somebody else told her. She'd come to him and he'd have to apologize, and he didn't intend to do that. He didn't owe her an apology. He did owe her something else, though. And that bothered him like an itch in the middle of the night. An itch he couldn't scratch. Ed flipped the sign so it read Open, unlocked the door and got out the cash box. The Book Nook was ready for business. Not that business was ready for it. Three years ago, when he first came here, he'd suggested to Miss LidaSue things might pick up if she had a new
sign.

pale hand liver-freckled as a trout, and paused at her office door. "I made the one we have. It is perfectly good."

He felt frost in the air fall to his desk. It was as though he'd opened a very large and deep freezer. Hell, he thought. That sign was a disaster from day one, but he didn't say anything else. He didn't mean the store needed something in neon, just a sign you could read. The letters B and N had faded so the words read "ook ook."

At least once a week kids on the phone giggled and finally blurted out, "Is this the ook ook? Ook Ook," they barked like seals. "Ook, Ook."

He counted out ten dollars in change, then decided what the heck and clinked in another ten. It was a Friday and he felt good. Maybe somebody would come in for a couple rolls of cellophane tape or some wrapping paper, though it wasn't likely. The tape was so old it broke when you tried to pull it and as for wrapping paper, who wanted a sheet that was faded on the folds or so dusty it made you sneeze spreading it out?

He slammed shut the cash drawer with a hard clank, and then took a damp rag from the workroom and wiped the counter. The counter was covered in the same thirties green as the floor and walls. Looked like the lobby of a bus station, he thought, but after his remark about the sign, he didn't say anything. Today Miss LidaSue could lump it or leave it.

Probably she wouldn't even notice. She stayed in her office more and more, and if she checked behind him, it was at ten when he went next door for coffee. Sure, he could bring a thermos like she did, but God, he had to get out of this place or the gray and gloom would descend on him like a great glob of wet plaster.

He had been at work since 8:30 if he was on time, though lately it had been closer to nine when he flew in and hooked his coat on the rack with such force he was surprised it wasn't still flapping when she came in.

If she felt his hurried opening, she never said anything, just the nod, her "Good morning," and leaving a trail of soap and mothballs as faint and distinct as glue, tip-tapped in her old lady lace-up heels to her office.

Half the store was stocked with Bibles and Bible school supplies, and the first thing Ed had to do each June was hang out the red and yellow banner: VBS. Vacation Bible School. In his mind, he made other words for it. Very Bad Stuff. Or Vagrant Birthday Suit or Varnish Blue Skies.

The banner was faded with letters cut from calico and ironed on. Ed was sure it was one of Miss LidaSue's little projects. Like her dresses. He knew she made those. Every dress was made from the same pattern, designed, he was sure, by the first Pilgrim mother. Large collar, long sleeves, high neck. God, she could pose, *sans* brother and pitchfork, for Southern Gothic if you added her little lunch in a basket and her purse, flat and black as a book. A very serious book. She felt one had to uphold one's profession. It was probably the bookkeeping ledger, but she did carry a book, and she didn't say anything when he read behind the counter, where he did most of his working hours. How long did it take to flip a sign card over? Open a cash register? Lock or unlock a door? Dust once a week? He couldn't rearrange the display windows, because the fabric had faded everywhere except under the books, and even their jackets were pale and gray. Didn't she know people wanted new books? Not Bible stories and *Webster's Dictionary* and the *Fannie Farmer Cookbook*?

Lately he read books from the public library two blocks down, a new building of yellow brick with a fountain out front. The local newspaper still got letters about the fountain and at least once a month printed one. Some irate citizen had told the county commissioners the fountain was a flagrant display of their total disregard for taxpayers' money when it was installed, and now "certain" people were bathing their babies in it and leaving dirtied diapers beside it on the courthouse lawn, which certainly said a lot about the state of affairs within.

Ed loved the letters. Sometimes he read them aloud in an irate voice to his daughter Katie, who lay on her bed and laughed. Sometimes she drew her legs up, she laughed so hard. Her face got pink and her eyes shone like blue buttons. He loved it when she laughed.

She laughed when he mimicked Miss LidaSue, held guffaws in her cheeks like candies and rocked. "She's a friend of Mama Rose's," Katie would say finally. "Don't let her see you do this. She'd have a fit."

Mama Rose. His mother-in-law Rose. His long-lost wife Cedora's mother, Katie's grandmother. Now there was a woman who could take the world, put it on a string and win a yoyo contest. And he'd applaud her. When somebody saves your life, you don't forget it. Not if you're Ed Swink. Not if you know who bakes your bread and hands you the butter, then a silver knife to spread it.

Ed dusted the pictures on his desk. Cedora at seventeen. Myrtle Beach. She always looked good in a bathing suit. Cap and gown. Cedora holding Katie ... a fat, bald kewpie doll of a baby and Cedora, head bent close as if she whispered secrets. Katie said sometimes she heard her mother's voice. Always at night and it woke her.

Ed didn't hear her. He saw her. In crowds. He saw the shine of her hair, the shape of her head, her profile always deep in the throng, and no matter how hard he pushed to get to her, saying "Excuse me" or "Pardon me" and called her name, he never got there in time. When the crowd thinned, when they'd burst through the wide doors of the mall or an auditorium and streams of people branched out in a dozen different directions, Cedora was gone. Gone as that day. Gone.

Next he dusted Katie's pictures in her gown and crown. Her grandmother's doings again. Little Miss Pageant. Junior Miss Pageant. Miss Teen Pageant. Rose knew how to raise a winner. And Katie seemed to bloom in the competitions. She loved the dresses, the dance classes, trucking to Atlanta or Richmond or Memphis.

Ed thought somewhere in some place, Cedora might see Katie on a news clip or in a newspaper and call them, come home. He always thought he saw her in the crowds. How he hurt so badly when he lost her, he felt carved out of ice. He ached. An ache he lived with like a shadow, a shadow that could rip him down the middle with a memory, make his legs shake in longing.

Rose said, "Katie can have Cedora's room. You take the guest room. When she wants to come home ... if she can." Ed heard the pain in her voice. "This is where she'll come."

But she hadn't. Not for three years, and now they had another life. Maybe Cedora did too.

Sometimes driving home, Rose and Katie would be so full of the pageant and winning, they bounced and sang, giggled and plotted the next one. "Not the pink sequined thing," Rose said. "That's out. Silver is in. Silver top hat and tights, singing 'Me and My Shadow.'" She hummed it, snapped her fingers.

Ed felt she had read his head in the dark. As Miss LidaSue would do in the daylight if he wasn't careful. How could she not know? Everyone else did. Everyone who lived in the real world, not one of thirty years ago. Rose said Miss LidaSue ran this store like her daddy was out to lunch or his Lion's Club meeting and would be right back. It was as if she waited for his step at the door, the jangle of the single rusted dusty bell. Listening. God, Ed thought, I know how she feels. He bet she heard the turn of his pages as he read. And he had read for three years. Mostly. When he wasn't selling Bible School Supplies, answering the phone (at least when the kids called it got him up to answer and their voices were fast and lively, even in their taunting "Ook ook"), or opening and closing the shop.

"How you handling the traffic?" some guy in the coffee shop would ask Ed every morning, and he'd play the game, wipe his forehead with his sleeve, say, "Our ten millionth customer just counted me out." Or "If traffic picks up any more, we're going to have to hire our own cop." Or deliveryman. Or somebodyjust to hold the door. Or he'd say he had just installed an automated credit card machine that all he had to do was call the numbers and it zipped through a charge in ten seconds flat. Or that robot, Ray the Robot, they had in their supply room had now cloned a family and they all beeped day and night getting the orders out. He had these running jokes with them. Jokes he knew never went out of the coffee shop. Jokes Miss LidaSue wouldn't understand. At lunch he just picked up his book, waved to her and walked out. Sometimes he had to wait until she turned from her desk, looked out the window and gave a quick bob of her head. She ate at her desk, he supposed. He never found any evidence she brought anything down to his desk nor the floor of the shop. And sometimes he came back late, just to see if she'd say anything. She never had. Now he stretched his hour more toward two, lingering in the coffee shop, at the library, walking the several blocks that used to be downtown. The stores had bent and torn awnings, glass fronts that reflected his tall figure as he went past, wide windows strewn with trash, broken and abandoned displays.

He started past an empty furniture store when he caught a glimpse of someone behind him and stopped, turned to look in the glass. That face. Those hollow eyes, wire-rimmed round glasses, thin cheeks. Had she followed him? Miss LidaSue? He moved. The face moved. Then stopped. Himself. Nobody else. He was alone on the street except for two people who stood in a serious and arm-gesturing discussion on a far corner. He hurried back toward the store feeling guilty, as though he'd been caught at something. Found out.

How could she not know? Didn't she read the papers? And it wasn't as though it was something he went out and asked for. They came to him. The owner of the chain had been in the coffee shop and asked where he could find Ed Swink, then waited until he came in. He was to be paid three times what she paid here, and the store was new. It was bright and clean and full of books ... new books. He couldn't wait. Already he worked some nights, checking in stock, getting the computer register set up, doing a real window display of best sellers. He wanted to shout at her: Do you see what a real window display is? They would open next week and he started Monday morning. Monday morning. The words had not sounded so good since he remembered.

So he walked and worded his resignation. "I've enjoyed working at the Book Nook" or "I'm sure you won't have any difficulty finding someone ..." Truth was, he thought she would. Maybe she wouldn't hire anybody. What she needed to do was close the shop. Go out of business. He thought that a hundred times. He told Rose so a hundred times. Sometimes late at night they sat at the kitchen table, drinking coffee, the radio on low, listening ... if the phone rang or there was a knock at the door.

"She'll never do it," he said.

Rose answered, "You know why."

"I can imagine."

"She'd have nowhere to go."

"You got it," Ed said.

When he got back from lunch, there was a note on his desk in her curled and rolled old cursive, "Call Penny at 783-1032." The number of the new bookstore at the mall.

He called and a cheery female voice rang, "Reader's Corner. How can I help you?" Penny. The girl they'd hired to work the checkout. She sounded like Cedora.

"Where do you want the Cliff Notes rack?"

"Near the back," he answered and glanced through the glass to see if Miss LidaSue listened. All he saw was her solid back, the steady board of her shoulders balancing her head on a thin, porcelain neck. She knew.

He wrote a note: "Thanks for everything," and propped it against his desk calendar. He left at two. She didn't even look up when the bell jangled.

The Country Girl's Story

Teeth

She was one of those country girls who came to town to work. They rode together from some far corner of the county in a mud-colored car caked with dust. The girls were dropped on a corner where they scattered to jobs in Roses or Woolworth's to sell hardwares or housewares. Occasionally one got a job in Belk's basement, where she sold rubbery-smelling shoes, bib overalls or measured out huge bolts of dry goods. These were girls who brought lunches in wrinkled and grease-spotted brown bags, treated themselves to a Coke in Levitt's Drug Store and fifteen minutes off their feet. They sat together in a back booth or huddled at a far table. There was something about them more than shyness or social ill ease. Were they simply unaware, or did they belong to a religion that permitted them to neither cut their hair, nor wear make-up or jewelry? No one knew.

Trula Hazelton was one of those girls. She worked in Roses, back of the store, dim corner. Housewares. Here she kept rows of baking sheets even, handles of dull iron skillets turned all one direction and sold glass replacement knobs for percolators or cards of silver-dollar- sized pot menders. Everything about Trula looked faded. Her cotton dresses were too long, hems barely missed being bobbed by her heels. Dresses that had probably belonged to an older sister or aunt or cousin who had worn them to this store to work at this same counter.

There was only a hint of blue in her eyes, and her hair had only the faintest touch of blond in its tight onion of a twist pinned at her neck. She smiled with her lips closed over huge white teeth. Horse teeth. Strong and healthy, but big and protruding. When Trula spoke she put her hand like a shield in front. She was nineteen but could have been forty. You knew how she'd look.

When Trula appeared in the hall outside Dr. Smitherman's office a minute before five that Friday, his nurse-receptionist, Judith Thrum, had almost closed and locked the door with the thick opaque glass. A bluish shadow stopped her.

"Do you have an appointment?" Judith asked.

Trula shook her head.

"He's finishing for the day," Judith said, hand on the brass knob.

"I ..." Trula stopped, swallowed. "I only want to talk to him." She glanced at the door's black lettering. "I heard he's good."

"You'll have to wait." Judith indicated the green sofa in the reception room.

The doctor wouldn't like it. He never liked drop-ins and especially not at five o'clock. His wife ran their house like he ran the office—by the clock. She didn't like holding dinner five, ten, fifteen minutes.

Dr. Smitherman frowned deep gray lines on each side of his mouth: an even darker one streaked across his forehead. He bent over a patient stretched in a chair, held a metal band around a hardening amalgam filling.

"She says she only wants to talk to you," Judith said. She had a nervous habit of running her fingers over the strand of baby pearls she wore over the high collar of her uniform. Pearls that belonged to her grandmother and she'd had them restrung. Pearls she wore daily like the perfume she ordered from New York twice a year, never told anyone the name, nor what shop special blended.

"Who is she?" Dr. Smitherman's patients were for the most part people in his social set, bridge partners, golfing buddies, neighbors, neighbors' children ... occasionally someone from the building, one of the lawyer's offices, internist down the hall, once in a while a maid or secretary.

"I think she works at one of the dime stores," Judith said.

Dr. Smitherman let a little grin pull the corners of his mouth. "I didn't know you ever darkened the door of such places," he teased.

The patient, a bald man with large feet in cordovan wing-tip shoes, grunted. He didn't want to be forgotten.

"At least once a year," Judith said. "Christmas. I buy bedroom slippers for my nieces. And there are times when I've run out of stockings." Stockings she mail-ordered too, from the same place she had her uniforms custom made.

Dr. Smitherman snapped the band off the patient's tooth, laid his instruments on the table and pushed it away. The bald man stood and shook himself like a huge dog. Judith removed the white bib and brushed his shoulders. "You're none the worse for wear," she said. "Think you'll live?"

The patient grumped, smoothed his hair and took the jacket Judith handed him from the rack where she'd hung it on a wooden hanger.

"Floss, and I'll see you in a year," said Dr. Smithereen. "Six months if you don't."

"Umph." The patient took his hat, yanked it down on his head and left.

Trula stood in the reception room where Judith had left her. "He'll see you now," she said and showed Trula in. She began to close the blinds, turn off lamps, straighten magazines on the tables.

Dr. Smitherman put Trula in the chair, where she lay stiff as wax and looked even more faded and bleached under the lights.

"There's not a thing wrong with your teeth," he said. "You got good healthy teeth and gums."

"I want them out," Trula said.

"But there's nothing wrong with them. I can x-ray to make sure, but you shouldn't be having any trouble."

"They don't hurt," she said. "I just want them out."

Dr. Smitherman put his hand on the arm of the chair. "I don't like to pull healthy teeth when there's no reason."

"I made up my mind," Trula said. She clamped her lips a hard navy blue line over the very white and extremely large teeth.

"Make her an appointment," he said, turning to Judith. "Next Friday at five."

He helped Trula stand. She blinked and rocked on her feet, then steadied.herself. "But," Dr. Smitherman continued, "I'd encourage you to think it over. At your age ... and nothing wrong with the teeth. A lot of people would give anything to have teeth that strong and healthy.

Next Friday at five Trula was there, standing like a scarecrow before the door.

"I made up my mind," she said. "I want them all out."

Dr. Smitherman sighed, outlined the procedure for her—four teeth at a time, one side at a time, leaving the last four until he had made impressions, ordered dentures and would place them in.

Trula left each week, cheeks packed hard with cotton sponges and her account up to date, paid with clean, tightly rolled bills.

Dr. Smitherman shook his head at each perfect tooth he pulled. He laid them out in a gleaming row with blood wound round them like threads. Trula never made a sound. Not a breath of pain escaped, though she stiffened each week in the chair before the needle of Novocain went in. She left looking sore and drained, thin, more like a February cornstalk than ever.

One Friday she had a blush to her cheeks. Rouge? Judith decided that's what it was. The next week, tiny earrings winked from each lobe. Well, Judith thought, what next? She began to consciously look for changes, differences each week.

A new blouse. Trula wore a fresh new blouse of cornflower blue the next week. Shoes with a little lift of heel.

Judith heard their clack as Trula left, then the elevator doors glide shut. The building had an elevator operated by an individual. The same person who'd been with both the building and the elevator forever, Judith thought. At least longer than the fifteen years she'd worked for Dr. Smitherman. Nedean. No one ever called him anything but that. The name embroidered in red above his gray uniform pocket. She'd never heard his last name. Nedean. Surely it was two words and somebody wrote it wrong, but each uniform was the same.

Nedean wore a brace on one leg and pulled the other when he walked, like it was longer and he had to keep tugging so it could keep up; most of the time he sat on a green stool beneath the elevator panel. He insisted on opening and holding the door for every female who used the elevator, acted gallant, stretched his arms and bowed a little. He always spoke, "Good morning," or "Good night now," and sometimes Judith thought if she closed her eyes and listened to only the voice, no picture, the person inside Nedean was extremely handsome.

When Judith heard the elevator close after Trula left each Friday, she realized Nedean must wait for her. Anyone else in the building after five walked down.

"Your girlfriend," she told Dr. Smitherman the next morning, "has a boyfriend."

"Who?" He held x-rays up to light, squinted.

"I'll never tell," she said and glanced over her shoulder as she let the next patient in.

"Who?" Dr. Smitherman tapped a filling.

"Worried somebody's making time with your girl?"

"You know, I wish I'd taken pictures," Dr. Smitherman said. "The way that girl looked before and now with all the gum work. I reconstructed that mouth. I could have done a presentation for the convention. Before and After. You wouldn't know it was the same girl."

Judith handed him the mirror.

That Friday Trula came in with a new haircut. Medium length. A feeble attempt at curls. Curls that sagged and drooped, looked limped and dispirited. Curls the color of dead leaves. The cut, Judith thought, did soften her face. "I like your hair."

Trula smiled, covered her mouth with her hand. Judith thought she heard half a giggle.

That week when Dr. Smitherman pulled the last teeth and placed in dentures, he and Judith stood back to see how Trula looked.

"Smile," said Dr. Smitherman.

Trula shook her head.

"It won't hurt," he said. "I know your lips feel a little numb, but give it a try."

Trula gave a slant of a smile and glint of new teeth. She'd had her hair cut more. A pageboy, with neat, blunt ends. It gleamed and framed her face. She wasn't pretty, but she had strong features. If she'd smile, Judith thought, that would make the difference.

That final Friday, Trula came for her fitting. Dr. Smitherman whittled and seated her teeth, made her bite down again and again, put his fingers behind each jaw, looked her full in the face.

"Smile," he said.

Trula's lips trembled, hesitated.

"I think there's somebody waiting for you in the hall," Judith said.

Trula giggled, her hand went up, then came down. Her eyes looked blue, face pink ... almost pretty as she smiled. She held out her hand. A chip of a ring winked.

"Well." Dr. Smitherman took her hand. "Congratulations. I never know what's going on around here." He looked at Judith.

"That's wonderful," she said.

"No pay this visit." Dr. Smitherman waved her money away. "A wedding present. This visit's on me."

Trula smiled white and wide and unafraid.

"That a girl. Keep it up." Dr. Smitherman took her elbow, helped her toward the door. "Keep it up."

Judith pulled the blinds, adjusted sofa pillows, turned out lamps. It was five-thirty-five.

Dr. S. closed his leather appointment book, slipped on his jacket—a Harris Tweed his wife chose. He looked in the mirror above his desk, squared his shoulders. "What she doesn't know," he said, "that boy would have done the same thing if she'd never had the first tooth pulled."

Three Women's Story

An Historic Event in Heritage Hills

My yard had been chosen for the big event because we had the largest fenced area. "Why a fence?" I asked Lou Latrelle when she called with the dubious honor.

"To keep the kids out," she said. "And of course to keep the customers confined to one area and under surveillance."

"Surveillance?" I said. "What kind of customers do you think we'll have?"

"You never know, she said. "And these days you can't be too careful. Why, I've heard of people who are yard sale professionals. Collectors. They'll come at the crack of dawn if they think they're going to get a bargain ... something cheap ... something for nothing. And they steal. It's better to be a little careful than worry about it later."

Lou Latrelle had organized the Heritage Hills Garden Club six years ago and had been president for the first five. This year I was vice president and in charge of fundraising. The spaghetti supper last month ended sixteen dollars in the red, so the yard sale was our last resort.

We were raising funds to buy flowering pear trees for both sides of Martha Washington Drive, azaleas and bulbs for the brick entrance area. The area was barren even of grass, which grew sparse and patchy ... much to Lou Latrelle's chagrin. It needed reseeding, fertilizing, maybe even sodding. "It needs love and care and attention," Lou said, like she was speaking of a sick, strayed or homeless animal. "It's the first thing anyone sees when they come into this development and certainly doesn't live up to its name." She sounded like Heritage Hills ought to have red, white, and blue flags flying, Eagle lanterns and some plantings as American as apple pie.

"Why not cherry trees?" I'd asked at the last meeting. "What's wrong with cherry trees?"

Lou gave me a look that would wilt anything but the most hardy. "Next spring." Lou spread her arms wide enough to embrace an elm. "All of Martha Washington Drive will be adrift in snow blossoms."

I giggled. Lou could be lyrical without trying. Before I took over the monthly newsletter, Lou had written it in rhyme.

"What about Abigail Adams Lane?" I asked, looking after my own home front.

"Apple trees are planned for Abigail," Lou said. "According to the neighborhood master plan. That's on next year's schedule. Pink boughs of fragrance ..."

"Crab apples," I mumbled on the way home. Lou meant well, but the way she went about things irritated everyone. She was the most uptight person in the world when it came to the lawns and landscape of Heritage Hills. She was the type to tell tulips they had to march in rows and all bloom at the same time, same height. Too bad she had to live in the same block as Joe and Judy Wheatley.

"If we wanted to adopt dandelions as the neighborhood flower," I told my husband Harvey, "Joe Wheatley could furnish enough for the next fifty years."

The Wheatley yard was the worst in Heritage Hills, and Joe's workshop spilled from their carport onto the drive and even into the side yard. The joke was that he was secretly a mad inventor or on contract for NASA.

"If only he'd call it sculpture," I said. "Maybe everyone, Lou especially, would feel better. Or we could say we'd established the Heritage Hills branch of the Modern Museum."

Joe Wheatley was actually the original Mr. Nice Guy Neighbor. He was an electronics whiz, fixed half the stereos, HiFis, VCRs, TVs, and garage door openers in the neighborhood and never charged a cent. Nobody could be nicer, even if he did happen to avoid lawn mowing with a passion and seemed to have a talent for growing dandelions. Maybe he was doing a crossbreeding program with them, we joked, because his yard was one big fuzzy field.

"Maybe he's got talents the rest of us haven't discovered," my husband Harvey said, "or stock in Weed-be-Gone."

Like the rest of the neighbors, we hauled home on a regular basis tons of fertilizer with weed controls built in or kept a regular supply of spray on hand.

The pear tree project was Lou's idea and we could see, through her eyes, a model neighborhood. Heavenly smelling and the picture of a model American suburb. If only the yard sale could come up with enough funds.

Six-thirty the morning of the yard sale, I awoke to a milling crowd under my bedroom window. It had rained the night before and in the mist, all those hooded and rain-coated people looked ghostly. I screamed.

Harvey shot from bed so fast he hit his toe on a chair and let out a yell that brought in the kids, Joanie and Fredrick.

"What happened?" Joanie yawned, trailing Raggedy Ann. "Who are all those people?" Joanie climbed onto the dresser, looked out the window. "What are they doing in our yard?"

Harvey hopped on one foot.

"Was there an accident?" Joanie asked.

"It was no accident." I hunted for my jeans, sweatshirt, sneakers. "It's the yard sale."

A woman wearing a beach hat decorated with purple alligators poked her face near the window. "Is this 1209 Abigail Adams Lane?"

Harvey dashed under the sheets.

"The sale doesn't start until eight." I disappeared into my sweatshirt.

The woman carried an expandable shopping bag, two umbrellas, a thermos and her lunch. "If I wait until eight, all the good stuff will be gone."

"What good stuff?" Harvey groaned, standing beside the bed wrapped in a sheet.

"Everybody can wait until we have breakfast. I insist."

"Well." The woman backed away from the window. "Pardon me." She took a folding stool from somewhere, sat and unwrapped her sandwich. "I brought my breakfast with me, thank you." The rest of the pros held their places like statues. Two or three left, saying they'd be back later and it had better be worth it.

"Get over here quick," I yelled at Lou Latrelle over the phone. "It's panic time. There's an angry mob at my door."

"Window." Joanie sat cross-legged on the dresser making up Raggedy Ann's face with my eye shadow and lipstick and hosing her with perfume. I swung Joanie down, and putting on my shoes, stumbled toward the kitchen where Harvey, still wrapped in his sheet like Caesar, scrambled eggs at the stove.

A man in a red polo shirt fingered a copper mold he'd taken off my wall. "How much for this?"

"It's not for sale," I snapped. "And please wait outside. Please." I felt for the coffee pot, poured myself a cup.

On his way out, the guy picked up a mug from the counter, wanted to know if it was in a set of six.

"No," I said and locked the door.

"Who was that guy?" Harvey asked. "He told me basil was good in scrambled eggs and he's right. Have some." He forked me a bite.

Joanie and Fredrick were outside in their pajamas. I could barely see them in the mist, but I heard the swing set creaking.

On the patio two women uncovered plastic from some of the boxes brought over last night, sorted through them. One had a music stand under her arm, the other a throw rug over her shoulder and a fur piece around her neck that had almost eaten itself down to a fuzzy string.

They pulled a pair of ice skates from a box, inspected an aquarium for leaks.

"Who unlocked the gate?" I asked Fredrick. He had the dog by her neck and tugged her toward the tree house. I climbed the ladder, got both of them down and told him to go see his father about some breakfast. "And get dressed ... both of you," I said.

I told the women we weren't open for business yet and they'd have to wait outside the gate until eight. Lou had been right after all to insist on using a fenced yard for the yard sale. I had to give her credit.

"This is certainly not the way to treat customers," the women muttered, but I noticed they waited.

I hollered for Joanie and started to relock the gate when Lou came flying up. Judy Wheatley panted behind, still in hot curlers, her nightgown showing beneath her dress. Lou dressed like Sunday, but her hair wasn't combed in the back and her lipstick went uphill on one side. The crowd cheered as they pushed through.

"How much longer is it going to be?" asked a man cradling a toy poodle. "I got three more of these things to go to today and gotta be on my way."

I sat Joanie on the gate and told her not to get down until I said so.

"What if I fall?" She licked jelly toast.

"Don't you dare," I told her and stationed Fredrick at the bottom. He wore one cowboy boot, hiking shorts, and one of Harvey's t-shirts that said: "America, Love it or Leave it."

By seven-thirty we had the tables up, booths around the yard. Harvey had the balloon concession going. "A quarter each?" he said. "What do you think?"

"Lou said fifty cents at the meeting." I glanced in Lou's direction.

Lou Latrell's card table in the corner of the yard looked like she'd robbed a china shop. Glasswear, ceramics, costume jewelry ... every dish sparkled. "It hurts my eyes to look." I shaded them with my hand.

Judy Wheatley's table at the opposite end of the yard was the wildest assortment of wires, old TV sets, odd-size speakers and stereo tapes—a real assortment. Judy's booth got Lou going first thing.

"Are you going to allow that bunch of junk to ruin our whole yard sale?" Lou asked. "Who in his right mind is going to buy any of that? You couldn't give it away. I certainly hope she doesn't expect the club to pay to have it hauled off when this is over."

Judy overheard Lou and blasted back, "I'll have you know this is a lot of expensive equipment and in demand by a lot of people."

Lou marched back to her own booth with her nose tilted like a teakettle.

"You ought to hold the next garden club meeting in Joe Wheatley's garage," Harvey said. "It's probably the cleanest place in the neighborhood."

He whooshed up a balloon, wrung its neck with string and handed It to Joanie. "For minding the gate."

We had the clothing corner, a wire strung between two trees, organized. And toys for sale in the very back, by the sandbox to keep kids out of the way.

Harvey, who had exchanged his sheet for a pair of paint-decorated shorts, had coffee and sodas going in the food concession.

A couple of men checked out the used camping equipment, picked up one water ski and a unicycle with a flat tire.

Crowds streamed in and out all morning. Things went smoothly, especially after such a bad start. At noon, I bought a sandwich from Sue Saunders at the Bake Booth. "I'm over here." Or "Here I am, dear." Leonard kept carting off boxes and Lou started to re-price pickle dishes with a sour expression.

Only minutes after Leonard and Joe left, Lou let out a scream. We all stopped dead still.

"It's gone," she screamed. "My wedding ring. It's gone."

Lou wrung her naked hands and cried, "It's been stolen."

We tried to calm her, searched the grass around, under, over, and in front of her booth. We lifted every pickle dish and ashtray twice to see if it was underneath. We examined a dozen times each pin and earring to see if somehow her wedding ring had gotten mixed in with the other jewelry.

When it couldn't be found, Lou insisted we call the police. Fredrick and Joanie filled balloons with water and let one go from the tree house. It hit a man rolling off one of the snow tires from Judy Wheatley's booth.

"I'm going to sue," he shouted.

"Did he pay for that tire?" Joe asked and Judy couldn't remember. Harvey went after him. The police seemed to think Lou's ring had gotten mixed in with the costume jewelry and was sold by mistake. There was nothing they could do, so they browsed around the yard sale.

Lou was in such a state, someone had to help her home. She kept repeating, "Somewhere out there is a woman wearing an eight hundred dollar diamond ring she bought for a dollar."

One of the policemean bought the set of ladies' left-handed golf clubs; the other an unframed wildlife print, *Bluebirds Nesting*.

After everyone had taken their tables down, left all the unsold stuff in our garage "for the next sale," Harvey and I sat on the patio with drinks.

The yard looked like a herd of circus elephants had done the hustle. There were three snow tires still stacked by the tree, a pile of broken lawn furniture, some bicycle parts, a mildewed pup tent and enough paper cups and napkins strewn to call a clean-up committee.

"The club made over five hundred dollars," I said. "That's more than enough for the pear trees. Martha Washington Drive should be a true burst of glory next spring."

Harvey closed his eyes to keep from seeing the ruined yard. The grass might never recover. There were mud puddles from the foot traffic and water balloons. Someone had spilled a can of green paint across the walk.

"I vote you spend the extra money on a plaque commemorating this historic event." Harvey lifted his glass. "On the sixth of June in the year ..."

"Friends and neighbors gathered to beautify, protect, and preserve," I added.

"I don't think Lou is going to be very happy about any of this," Harvey said. "Somehow she blames us for the loss of her ring, and I would be surprised if she doesn't think it's the responsibility of the Heritage Hills Garden Club to contribute toward her loss."

"You mean it wasn't insured," I said.

"Not according to Leonard. He handles all those things and had let the policy lapse ... he thought. He couldn't remember and Lou was in no state to think straight."

"There go the pear trees," I said. "And the apple trees and the bulbs for the entrance. What does that leave us?"

"Joe Wheatley told me he's planning to build a greenhouse with the money Judy got from the sale of his electronic equipment," Harvey said.

"With his green thumb in gear." I laughed. "We'll have this neighborhood abloom in no time."

"Long live the Dandelion Farm," Harvey said, and we toasted friends, neighbors. Joe Wheatley, Leonard and Lou Latrelle, all the members of the Heritage Hill Garden Club.

"And whoever out there got an eight-hundred-dollar diamond ring for a dollar," I said. "America is still the land of opportunity."

Going to Graceland

Epilogue

If these Seekers fail to find The Rapture in this life, it is not the fault of the author. She has done her best to give them free rein, which they promptly took in their teeth without letting her get a word in sideways. They charged off on their own, lickety split, hotfooted to Graceland and came dragging themselves back. But they've been. They've been there. All that's left is living day to day, prayer when the devil gets hard on their heels and twelve months until next August. Pilgrims, lost and found. Pilgrims, all.

Brief Biographical Sketch

Ruth Moose has published stories in the *Atlantic, Redbook, the new renaissance, North American Review, Alaska Quarterly Review* and many other places. Her stories also appeared in publications in England, Sweden, Denmark and South Africa. Some stories were broadcast on NPR. She has had Pushcart Awards, a MacDowell Fellowship, an NEA grant and won teaching awards while on the faculty at UNC Chapel Hill. *Going to Graceland* is her fourth collection of short stories. She has published two novels, *Doing it at the Dixie Dew* and *Wedding Bell Blues,* with St. Martin's Press. She has also published six collections of poetry, including, most recently, *Tea and the Librarian*.

Made in the USA
Middletown, DE
28 January 2019